SHADOW WITCH

The Shadow Winged Chronicles: A Novella

JILLEEN DOLBEARE

ICE RAVEN
PUBLICATIONS

The Shadow Winged Chronicles

Shadow Lair: Book .5
Shadow Winged: Book 1
Shadow Wolf: Book 1.5
Shadow Strife: Book 2
Shadow Witch: Book 2.5
Shadow War: Book 3

*Forthcoming

Shadow Witch
The Shadow Winged Chronicles: Book 2.5
Jilleen Dolbeare

Copyright © 2022
Editor: Cissell Ink
Cover Designer: Crimson Phoenix Creations
Interior Art: Rose Rasmussen

All rights reserved. No part of this book may be reproduced, scanned, or distributed in any form including digital, electronic, or mechanical, including photocopying, recording, uploading, or by any information storage and retrieval system without prior written consent of the author except for brief quotes for use in reviews.

I dedicate this book to the people that have supported and encouraged me along the way. My writing friends, my "masterminds," and my regular friends that keep encouraging me, thanks! You know who you are! To my niece, Baylee Rose who read everything, kept me focused, made suggestions, and for her brilliant art. And to all my alpha and beta readers. Thank you all!

Foreword

First, thanks for picking up this book, I hope you enjoy it! It's always tricky when a non-native writer writes about a native character. Living among the Inupiaq in Barrow, Alaska, I felt I could bring a native character to life while incorporating native Alaskan folklore.

Since Piper, having lived outside of her culture, gets to learn along with the reader about her background and traditions, I hope I will be forgiven for any unintentional slights as a non-Alaskan Native. I love the rich history and traditions of the Inupiaq and learning their folklore has been enlightening and difficult since until very recently (in anthropological terms) they were passed down orally.

I have used recordings from oral tellings; conversations from Inupiat friends, colleagues, and neighbors; tales from the Arctic Inuit peoples, and other Alaskan Native folklore to create Piper and her world. I hope that the stories I've spun will bring the folklore of the north alive. Good reading everyone!

Chapter 1

The eagle swooped down on me. I shrieked and ducked before I realized it was an ally. I breathed a sigh of relief when I recognized the Stellar's sea eagle, one of the leaders of the shadow winged Orca Clan. He dropped a message on top of my red crossover. When he back winged, the blast from his eight-foot wingspan swirled my hair and blinded me for a moment. I remembered my manners and yelled, "thank you," with a wave as he rose above the trees and flew away. We'd been sending messages this way lately since our trouble with the police and the Silla Corporation had left us paranoid about spies.

I couldn't reach the paper, so looking around to make sure that no one could see, I used magic to push it over the roof of the car and into my hand. It was a rolled-up piece of notebook paper. I recognized Piper's handwriting.

Piper was my best friend—a Raven Clan shapeshifter whose father was Raven himself. Yes, that Raven. My best friend was the daughter of a Native totem, a god if you will. It was new knowledge to both of us, and frankly, I was still freaked out about it. I'd known him for nearly all my life and thought of him as my second dad, then this. It was mind blowing.

"Bran, we're meeting at The Meeting Room at 8." She followed that with an address on Old Seward. I shoved the note in my pocket and continued to walk to my house.

I was late, and the realtor frowned. Probably for more than my tardiness. She wasn't used to having the seller involved this much, I could tell. But I was still attached to the house, even if I couldn't stand to live in it anymore. I sighed and explained it to her again. "No, there is nothing structurally wrong with the house."

I couldn't tell her that a group of werebears had defiled it and scared me so badly I never wanted to stay alone in it again—this place that had been my sanctuary.

"Why are you selling it below market value?" she asked again, although I'd told her twice why.

"I want it to sell fast, so I can move on."

We walked through the house, and I told her what I thought were its best selling points. I'd had the interior completely redone—paint, new windows, lots of wall repair, and new flooring. The house was practically new again.

"You can get a lot more," she said again. I realized that underselling it cut into her bottom line, but I had to get out of my parent's house, and I needed this to sell yesterday to do it. I had already found a few prospects, but I didn't want to make an offer until this house was off my hands.

"Be positive, maybe under selling it will bring in a price war," I said, sort of snottily. She was wearing on my nerves.

I'd been in my parent's house since being shot multiple times following the supernatural battle at Fred's. I'd recovered, finally, and I was itching to be back in my own place. I loved my parents, but they were too deeply involved in my life—it was *exhausting*.

Finally, the walk through was finished, and the realtor was on her way with pictures and descriptions to add to her listing.

I went back to my store, the Lunatic Fringe, a book and novelty store in Anchorage, Alaska. The store was mainly aimed at tourists, but I had a rare book clientele that stretched worldwide. I had a knack for finding rare and out of print folklore books. I did well. Well enough, I was comfortable.

My manager greeted me as I entered. The store was empty. The summer tourist season had ended in September, and now that the cold and dark were approaching, the store mainly attracted locals looking for gifts or oddities. I had those.

Since no one was there, I headed to the back to work on my other pastime—research. Since Piper and I were deeply involved in this clandestine war against her uncle, a god who represented Eagle in Alaskan Native myth, I was constantly searching for any information about him, his powers, and his allies. And since a lot of Native myth and folklore were oral, it was hard to find. I'd probably exhausted all I *could* find, but I constantly searched.

I finished my latest bout of research with another list of obscure books, pushed back from the computer, and sighed. This was going nowhere. I stood and stretched my back. As soon as I was done with physical therapy and weekly doctor visits, I was having Raven heal me *completely*. This healing at human speed was for the birds, ha! The birds! I chuckled to myself at my own stupid joke.

I'd been taking Piper's advice and giving more responsibility over the shop to my manager. Since she was here today, I packed up my stuff, grabbed my list of books and put on my jacket. I needed to go to the library to see if they had any of these. The Anchorage library had a great section devoted to books on Alaskan Native folklore, and it was the best place to find things I couldn't find anywhere else.

Jed the swan was meeting me at the library today. He was in hiding. Eagle knew about him and that he'd been a spy in his camp. If Eagle's people found him, it wouldn't go well for him, so he moved around a lot and stayed busy. He was a student at the local university, although he had to switch to online to avoid being captured again.

I pulled around back and parked. Jed was meeting me by the silo part where the Alaska Native collection used to be stored. He was waiting by the elevator. Jed was tall, better-than-average looking, light eyed, with reddish blonde hair. You couldn't tell by looking at him he was a quarter Inupiaq, but he spoke fluently.

"Hi," he said simply when I got close enough.

I smiled at him. I liked him well enough; I just wasn't attracted to him as much as he wanted me to be. "Hi back."

He had a backpack slung over one shoulder, but his laptop was tucked under his arm, so he must have been working before I showed up.

"You don't mind moving into the Alaska Collection?" I asked. He'd probably been set up elsewhere.

"No, it doesn't matter."

The part of the library that had housed the collection of Native books had been flooded a few years ago and the silo, or rotunda, as the library called it, was being redesigned. Everything else was housed upstairs until the remodel was completed. I was glad—the old part felt like being locked in a missile silo. I'd always been afraid to be trapped in it during an earthquake, then there was an earthquake, go figure. We had earthquakes almost daily, but the one that flooded the library had been big.

We set up, and I went to see what books on my list they had, if any. I got lucky and pulled three of the seven. I sat next to Jed and spread out my research material. He smiled at me but didn't make a move or pressure me to get closer or any of that male nonsense. It was refreshing. I was sort of an introvert, and the best way to turn me off was to pressure me to be more social than I wanted to be.

Before I got too involved in my work, I reached out with my senses to see what supernaturals were around. I could sense Jed, but only because he was within a five-foot radius of me, and his feel was only a gentle ripple on my senses. He wasn't very strong. He didn't even need to learn to shield. I pushed my senses past his texture and reached. We were deep in the library, and unless something very powerful and unshielded was nearby, I wouldn't be able to sense anything.

That's why I froze when a hot, fiery blaze lit up my senses. I immediately pulled back and slammed my shields down. That felt close—like in the library, close. My breathing sped up, and I whispered to Jed, "We're in trouble."

He looked up and frowned at me. "What's up?"

"Big magic. Here in the library."

We both packed up hurriedly. Piper had told me she could only feel me if she was within three feet of me when my shields were active. It was the same for her. So as long as we stayed away from people, no one should feel us. I started scanning the people nearby. I didn't recognize anyone, not that there was a reason I should recognize anyone.

I had a couple of tricks up my sleeve. I could zap people with slightly more force than a stun gun, throw a super-cooled ball of air, or a super-heated one. I'd developed a shield that could repel bullets and other weaponry for a time, and of course, block my magical signature. This was an upgrade for me. Before, when I'd first learned this, I had a tendency to knock out all electronics within about ten feet. I'd been working on fixing that. I was trying to upgrade my magical arsenal, as well. Nothing I had was currently lethal. It was all practical but hadn't helped us in our last battle.

We exited the Alaska Collection and headed for the exit nearest the parking lot. Jed and I scanned around for anyone we recognized or who looked suspicious. A flash of red caught my eye, and I saw someone I knew. She'd come into the store before and picked up a rare book she'd ordered about Raven. Her power was scary, strong enough she had to be a Sky Person, one of the ancient Native gods. I grabbed Jed's arm and pulled him behind a shelf. She knew me and I knew her. At least I knew her face and name, but nothing else about her.

Her last name sounded Inupiaq. I wasn't a native speaker, although I knew a few words and recognized a few more. I didn't know what it meant, if it meant anything. Jed might, though. I peered around the shelf. I didn't see her. "Come on," I whispered to Jed. We slunk through the shelves and headed toward the door. Just as I thought we'd made it, I saw her.

She was standing between a wall and a shelf, waiting. When I turned my head, I caught her eye, and we stared at each other for a moment. Then to be cheeky or because I was nervous, I threw a little finger wave and smirked at her. She folded her arms over her chest and frowned slightly. Rudely, she didn't return the wave. The first time I met her, she wore a meticulous business suit that fit her like a glove, showing off enviable curves. This time she wore another, same cut, same enviable curves. No suit should do that. I hit the crash bar on the door, and Jed and I fled into the fading autumn sun.

We made it into the parking lot; she hadn't followed. The tension in my shoulders eased some. I didn't know what her game was. If she was part of Eagle's syndicate, she already knew I wasn't Raven's daughter. I wasn't anyone worth noting in the scheme of things; I was just a plain old human. I wondered why she had stalked me here.

"Do you know her?" Jed asked when we reached my car.

I looked at him. "I know her name, and that she was interested in Raven before all the revelations occurred."

"What is it?" he asked, a troubled look on his face.

"Malina Itigiaq."

He shuddered visibly, and an oppressive feeling overtook me. My magic did that sometimes. I have visions or premonitions, and this one was a doozy. Almost like I knew what was about to come out of his mouth.

"Itigiaq is Inupiaq for weasel." He leaned on my car. "I think she *is* Weasel."

The truth felt like a punch to the gut, but I wasn't ready to accept it. "No, Weasel died in the wars. Raven said so."

"You felt that. I could feel it, too. I've seen her around with Eagle. She's not a lowly shadow winged. She's not human. That's what a Sky Person feels like. She felt like Salmon, blazing with power. Her name is Itigiaq, just like Raven is Tulugaq, and Eagle is Tiŋiakpak. That makes her Weasel."

I looked at him; his eyes seemed to change between grey and blue. Today they were grey. "Do you think she could be that Weasel? Raven's ex and Eagle's wife? Or someone that took over the totem?"

He shook his head. There was no way to know that without asking her or Eagle, and there was no way either of us was going to do that. She'd eat us for lunch. Her power dwarfed ours; we were the weakest of our team—barely even players. Jed had been spying for us; now the only thing he could do was fly messages, and swans weren't that common in Anchorage, so even that was limited.

We separated and hurried to our respective vehicles, still looking back. No red suit. Jed was probably heading back to his hideout. Somewhere with Fred. I turned back to my parent's house.

About halfway there, my phone rang. My heartbeat, which had finally slowed down after the library, ratcheted back up, and I jumped. I looked at my Bluetooth display. It was Jed. He must have forgotten something.

"Hello?" I answered, confused.

"Sorry. With the excitement, I forgot to ask. How about Friday night?" he asked timidly.

I felt a shock run through my system. He hadn't bothered me for a while about going out with him. I'd been too injured. I hadn't forgotten, per se, I'd just put it on the back burner of my mind. This wasn't the best time to ask, either. Weasel, if that's who she was, was up to something, and neither of us knew her agenda.

"Umm," I said, stupidly. I couldn't get out of this. I'd basically already agreed, and he was nice enough I didn't want to hurt him. "Sure. Can it be after seven? I'm closing."

"I can pick you up at the store if you want."

"That works. What are we doing?"

A moment of silence, I could hear a car blinker. "Yeah, sorry. How about a movie at the dinner theater at the Bear's Tooth?"

I hadn't done that for a long time. I was usually too busy or would rather pick up something to eat. "Sounds like fun." I hung up and groaned. I didn't want to do this, but I felt trapped by my own stupidity.

Chapter 2

An hour later, I left the house. Malina Itigiaq was heavy on my mind, but I didn't dare call Piper. We made sure to only talk about innocuous things on phones. I'd have to wait until I saw her at the meeting. Between her and the problems with Jed, my stomach churned. It might have been anticipating my physical therapy session, but this other stuff wasn't helping. I turned at the next light and headed to my appointment. That would keep my mind off things for a while. It took a lot of concentration and pain to get through one of those.

I was exhausted afterwards, so I headed home to rest for a moment and take a shower. I hoped that doing those two things would re-invigorate me. They didn't. I dressed and hauled myself back to my car. I'd been careful to put on makeup and do my hair, so I didn't look as exhausted as I felt. I knew Piper was worried about me, but I really was fine. It just took time.

We were all still dealing with the aftermath, and I don't mean just recovering. The police had been in everyone's business since. If they'd found the bodies, we'd be in hot water for the rest of our natural and unnatural lives. We'd been at Fred's when we were attacked by Eagle and his goons from Silla Corporation. Several, I don't know how many, but probably close to a hundred, black-clad supernatural soldiers dressed in high tech armor and armed to the teeth had attacked Fred's house looking for an ancient *were* making artifact that was hidden in Fred's panic room. They'd shot us up and blown up his house.

We'd given as good as we got. Fred and Raven were warriors, and they'd used their shapeshifting powers to annihilate the soldiers in their way. Piper and Fletcher too. I was just a human with some magic, but I'd done what I could. Most of my power was defensive and uncomfortable rather than lethal, though. The others that had helped us were also shifters, but we'd been out-manned, outgunned, and we'd lost. The bad guys got the artifact, I'd nearly died, and Fred's house was destroyed. I shuddered at the memory. I'd been shot multiple times and nearly bled out.

Fred and Piper took me to the hospital, while Raven had stayed behind and clouded the minds of the police until all the other members of our shadow army had removed the bodies and disappeared. It had been a feat worthy of a god, in my opinion.

I pulled into the parking lot of a commercial building in a strip mall. Lots of parking for other businesses, so easy to hide among the rest of the traffic. Still, I was shocked when I walked in, and the place was full. We'd really grown. That made me happy and wary at the same time. Quick growth meant it was hard to weed out the spies, and I knew we had to have some. The big guns in our group did their best, but I was the only one that could actually crack into someone's mind. I could feel the tension build. I was going to have to screen new people tonight. I frowned.

There was food and drink laid out, as there always was when shifters were involved. They had to keep shoveling food in because they spent so many calories every time they shifted. Tonight, it looked like sub sandwiches, chips, cookies, and pop, all of which were disappearing quickly. I grabbed a Coke from the table. It was warm. I frowned at it, concentrated, and soon a deep cold radiated from the can.

"Me next," a cheerful voice said behind me. I whirled around, smiling.

"You want me to hit you with a big chill?" I said playfully.

Piper rolled her eyes. "Nope, just this." She held out her can and sloshed it around. "It's warm. You can't drink warm Coke; it's against the law."

"Uhuh," I agreed.

I aimed my freeze ray at her can.

"Thanks!" She slurped loudly.

I cringed.

We stood there in companionable silence for a moment, drinking.

"Do you remember Malina Itigiaq?" I asked, after Piper came back from grabbing a sandwich.

"Yeah, the big power that came to the store in the suit."

"She was watching me at the library today."

Piper frowned. "What does she want from you?" she asked sharply. Even though it was a rhetorical question, I'd been wondering the same thing.

"I don't know." I could feel that pressure in my chest, my magic warning me about something. "I have a bad feeling."

"Shit," she said. "Do you feel like a vision is coming on?"

It was my turn to frown. "No, I don't think so. Just a general bad feeling about her." We were both quiet for a beat. "Jed says Itigiaq means weasel, and he's pretty sure she is *that* Weasel. Your dad's ex."

"That's why her name sounded so familiar. I need to work on my Inupiaq," she mumbled.

"Isn't Weasel supposed to be dead?" We both asked at the same time and then laughed.

"It's your job to find out. Your dad said she was, so ask him why she's turning up now."

"I wonder why he thought she was dead. Do you think she's a different Weasel?" she asked, her voice small.

"My gut says no, she's the same old one."

"Damn."

"Yup."

"I'll talk to him."

We both looked over to where her dad, Raven, stood talking to a small group of people. I couldn't tell who they were since their backs were to me. She probably wouldn't get him alone until after this thing, so I doubted my curiosity would be assuaged tonight. I looked around. Maybe Fred would know. He usually stood head and shoulders over the crowd, since so many of the shifters were Native and he was over six foot six, but I didn't see him.

That got me all in my head again. Did I want to see him because I could pick his brain, or because I just wanted to see him? Be near him? I shut it down.

"So, you were meeting Jed at the library?" Piper announced somewhere between a statement and a question. This was her way of trying to get me to fill in the dirt.

"Yes, but we weren't there very long before the whole Weasel thing."

She gave me a sidelong look. "You know what I'm really asking."

I sighed. "Fine. He asked me out for Friday. We're going to the Bear's Tooth after work."

"The Bear's Tooth, huh?" She smirked. Why did female friends try to match make when they were in a relationship?

I stopped that line of thought. It wasn't fair. Piper had spent her life so far trying to find someone she could share her true self with. She was happy. She just wanted me to be happy too.

"Yeah," I answered.

She looked at me more closely. "You should just tell him you aren't interested."

"But I should be," I said, vehemently. I took a long drink and finished the can. "He's cute, he's into me. I don't have to explain any of this…" I waved a hand to indicate the crowd, "to him. He's age appropriate, and he's chasing me, so I don't have to do much work. It should be perfect."

She nodded. "All true. But you and I both know you've got the hots for Fred."

One thing about Piper, she wasn't subtle. You always knew exactly what she was thinking. She accused me almost daily of reading her mind, but who had to? She was an open book.

I shook my head. "I could. True. But I am not going there."

"Why not?" she asked.

It was logical on the surface. We were both single, both adults, both attracted to one another. It was just not logical in the long term. I'd grow old and die in the blink of an eye to him. He'd already lived for longer than twelve millennia. He'd live forever if no one removed his head. Anything could kill me, and I had maybe fifty more years if I lived an average length of time for a female human. Plus, I'd age. He'd always be in his prime. "It just wouldn't work."

As I said that, I felt him enter the building. I turned. I wasn't the only one that noticed. Fred, maybe because of his size or the force of his personality, filled a room with his presence. Piper looked at me, then followed my gaze to him. She smirked.

"Look at that; lover boy is here."

"Stop, Piper, you know that teasing drives us both crazy."

"Yeah, so?" She finished her Coke and threw it in the trash. She brought us both another.

I slushed them up. She was right, Coke was best on the edge of being frozen.

Fred was making his way to us. I looked around for Fletcher. He was rarely far from Piper, but I didn't see him.

"Where's Fletcher?"

"He was doing something at the house. He said he'd be a little late," she said with a shrug.

Fletcher had just bought a beautiful new house for both of them to move into. Piper was wearing an engagement ring, although not on her finger, but on a heavy chain around her neck. Rings didn't do well on shifters. They got lost a lot. The chain helped her when she shifted. If she shifted into a wolf, it stayed on, but into one of her other forms, she could hang it on something so it wouldn't get lost.

Fred was almost to us.

"Ask him about Malina. I'll go grab Dad before that next group does," she said, and I saw what she meant.

A group was trying to break into the circle of people he was talking to. I nodded. She moved away, and Fred was in front of me, smiling.

"Hi." I smiled back. He made me nervous. I still wasn't sure if it was because he intimidated me, or because I liked him. But there it was. I straightened my spine. I might feel nervous, but I refused to look at it.

He greeted me.

Then, because I didn't want to talk about me, which he would ask about, I blurted out. "Do you know a woman named Malina Itigiaq?"

That got a violent reaction from him. Neither Raven nor Fred ever showed emotion or what they were thinking on their faces. But Fred jerked, and his face showed deep surprise.

He loomed over me. "Where did you hear that name?" He almost sounded like he was angry at me, but I knew that couldn't be. The unease I'd been feeling since I saw her earlier bubbled up, and my nausea returned. I sipped my Coke, forcing the nausea back.

"The first time I met her was at my store. She bought a book about Raven folklore. The second time was today. She followed me to the library. Both times she flared her power at me so I'd know she was a Sky Person." I watched his face while I spoke, but he'd regained control of his expressions.

He looked over at Raven. "What did she look like?" This was one of those questions that I hated to answer. These ancient beings were shapeshifters. They could appear to be anyone or anything they wished. I could describe her, but what did it matter? True, she may be using a form that they'd all know, but if she was, it was only to mess with their heads. She could be another being trying to pose as the original Weasel, or she could be playing some game we'd never guess altogether.

I wanted to say, "Really?" with all the sarcasm I could muster, but it seemed important to him, so I described her. "She's probably five-eight or nine, slender but shapely, long dark hair with a slight wave, golden skin, and luminous amber-colored eyes. She's breathtakingly beautiful."

Fred closed his eyes for a moment. He grabbed me around the top part of my arm and led me to a less crowded spot. He leaned in.

My heart sped up and for a moment; I thought he was going to kiss me. Big misinterpretation.

Instead, he hissed, "Weasel. You just described Weasel. She's supposed to be dead." Then he looked down at me and realized he was still clutching my arm. "Sorry," he whispered and let go. "I've got to go talk to Raven." He scanned the room.

"Piper is going to warn him and ask why he thought Weasel was dead."

"You knew it was her?" he asked, confused.

"Not until this afternoon. I knew her name from the store, and I knew she was big magic, but it was Jed that recognized that Itigiaq meant weasel. Then we put two and two together."

"You were with Jed?" he asked, a strange note in his voice. Then he cleared his throat and looked away.

"He was helping me with some research at the library," I said, although I don't know why I felt the need to explain. Fred and I weren't dating. We'd only thrown furtive glances at each other.

"Weasel is dangerous. Stay away from her."

"Like I have any choice," I snapped at him, annoyed. I wished I'd never met her.

"She makes Eagle look as sane as Mother Teresa," he continued.

If my words cautioned him at all about his stupid statement, he didn't show it. Plus, I had no idea how sane Mother Teresa had been, but she'd seemed caring, and I doubted the ability of any of the Sky People, Raven excepted, to care about anything human.

I was going to say something snarky, but he had already left me and was headed towards Raven. People cleared a path for him. Angry werewolf coming through, I thought and snickered to myself, the nerves getting to me.

Jed found me, and I looked at Fred nervously, worried he'd come back and find us together. Fred could eat Jed for lunch, both literally and figuratively. I had to remind myself there wasn't a reason for him to do so. We weren't together. Plus, Fred felt protective of the swan. I tried to relax some.

"Hey, Jed," I said.

He had a plate full of food, and he was wolfing it down as he walked. He swallowed. "Hey. Did you tell Fred about Weasel?"

I nodded. "Yes, he's going to go talk to Raven right now."

We stood in silence as he ate. Waiting. I continued to watch Raven, Piper, and Fred as they talked. People had cleared away from them since Fred had joined, and that amused me. Finally, Piper and Fred broke away and headed back to me. Raven went up to the podium and turned on the mic to start the meeting. The food was mostly gone.

"Good evening, everyone." The mic squealed, and the sensitive-eared shifters flinched. "Sorry about that." He adjusted something on a panel then came back. "We had a plan for this meeting, but some new information has just been presented to me, and I have to verify some things. Since it will change what we are going to do moving forward, we'll have to reschedule."

People were looking around curiously, but no one seemed upset or concerned. They went back to eating and visiting.

"The new meeting place will be sent to you by the usual method."

Nods from the crowd, then Raven turned off the mic and joined the group that had been trying to get his attention earlier. Jed and I joined Piper and Fred.

"So, what did he say?" I asked impatiently.

Piper looked up at Fred. He gestured for her to continue.

She took a deep breath and blurted, "The short version is no, he didn't know for sure that she was dead. He'd heard it from a reliable source. Yes, it would have been easy to fake a death back then. It is possible it's not her, but he thinks it is her. He's concerned because he'd been worried about another player, and this is a worst-case scenario."

I looked up at Fred for a confirmation; he gave one quick nod.

If I liked to swear, this would be the time for it. Instead, I said, "What do we do now?"

No one had any ideas.

This confirmation wasn't helping my exhaustion. I wished I could leave, but just as I thought that, Raven came to grab me. I had three new members that couldn't be vetted the usual way, and I needed to break into their minds, with their permission of course, and verify. I hoped I'd have the energy to walk out of here when I was done.

Friday morning, I rushed to work because I'd slept in. It wasn't usually that big a deal, but my manager was off for a few days, and since the store wasn't busy, I hadn't scheduled anyone else for opening or closing. I had someone for the middle part of the day in case I needed to do something or wanted a break. I was the boss, I shouldn't have to worry about being five minutes late, but someone might be waiting on me, and I hated the idea of that. I prided myself on punctuality.

I was half afraid I'd show, and Weasel would be waiting for me, but that was just fear, not truth. No one was there, and no one showed up until my help arrived after lunch. Once my employee started, I left for a while. I had some errands to run, and the realtor already had viewings scheduled for my house, which had my heart beating hard with nerves. I needed something to distract me and sitting at work with no customers wasn't helping.

To kill time and settle my nerves, I arranged to look at a new house. When I walked in, I knew it wasn't for me. The atmosphere was dark and oppressive. I didn't even finish the walk through.

Piper invited me over, since they were moving in soon, and she wanted my opinion on furniture. Fletcher had been doing some upgrading, although I don't know of what, the house was pretty much perfect.

I texted her I was on my way once I'd finished my errands. The house was stunning. It was on a forested five acres on the hill heading out of town to the south. It was large, not a mansion like Fred's had been, but good sized. It must have cost a couple of million dollars. I know Piper had said it was well out of her price range. It blended into the surroundings with wood and stone and a slate roof. I rang the bell.

"Hey," she said when she opened the door.

"Hey back." I entered the foyer, which was vaulted and well lit. A staircase rose up the right-hand side, and the foyer led to two rooms. One looked like a den and the other a formal living room. The floors were wide wood planks, except in the entry where they were stone. I'd hate to clean that. She walked me to the back. We sat at Fletcher's kitchen table, the only furniture in the house.

"Snacks?" she asked.

"Uh, no. I'm good."

She shrugged and grabbed a bag of chips from the cupboard. I shook my head. If I ate half of what she did, I'd have to be rolled to work every day.

"So, what's up, what help did you need?" I asked after the quiet stretched past my comfort zone.

"We are so busy with the coming war, and trying to stay off the radar, that I don't have time to worry about this huge house. I just don't know what to do next." She sighed. "It's so big, and it doesn't feel homey yet. It's cold and bright and loud."

"Huh." I looked around. Without carpet or furniture to absorb sound, it probably was loud.

Piper was in the same situation as me. Our homes had been violated by werebears, and we'd had to get them fixed up and sold. She'd already sold hers since she'd had time to get it on the market first. Being downtown, hers had sold fast and at the top of the market.

"You need rugs and furniture to help absorb sound," I said drily. She already knew this, so she gave me a look.

"Yeah, I know. I need help deciding on which ones." She opened her laptop and showed me a few she had bookmarked. We spent a couple of hours loading up her cart. This was not something she enjoyed doing. It wasn't at the top of my list either, but it was a great way to hang with your bestie because it was basically mindless. It also kept our thoughts off the coming war.

Finally, the pressure had built up too much. The bad feeling was sitting on my breastbone like a stone. "What are we going to do about Weasel?"

She looked at me strangely. "I don't know if we can do anything," she said after a minute. "We don't know anything about her."

"Yeah, and the stories that mention her are limited."

"We can look at the stuff we know about the animal. I know Dad has told me before that we take on the traits of the animals we represent."

I looked her up and down, and said, "That's true."

Piper scoffed. "Ha, ha, you are hilarious."

"Let's look at you." I held up a hand and started putting fingers down as I listed my points. "Pathological curiosity, check. Short attention span, check."

She interrupted me. "My attention span isn't short; I'm just easily distracted."

"Fine. High distractibility, check."

She rolled her eyes.

"High intelligence, check."

She looked at her fingernails, then buffed them on her shirt. "That's right. Keep going."

"Huge ego, check."

"Whatever." We both laughed.

"Love of shiny things to a high degree, check."

"That is true, I love my ring. It's very shiny." She pulled it out of her shirt, and we both admired it. It was white gold with a two-carat diamond, maybe more, it looked huge anyway. It had a bunch of smaller diamonds along the band. Extremely shiny. "But liking shiny things isn't a personality trait."

"It isn't? Then whoever wrote the rules never met you."

She cocked her head and grinned. "True."

"You are also bold, brave, courageous, and will wade into a fight without a thought."

"You really think so?" She was quiet for a moment. "I *do* think about it. The wading into a fight bit, and I'm scared. I just can't let injustice go."

"That's another thing. You have an overdeveloped sense of fairness. I don't know if that's a raven thing. You also have wolf traits, or they fit both animals. I don't know. That need to have a mate. I think that is from both of your animals."

"You don't have a need for a mate?" she asked. She knew me.

I also wished for my own happy ending, if any of us survived. Otherwise, I wouldn't be drooling over Fred like I was, or letting Jed take me out. I shrugged. "Point taken. I'll strike that off the list." I drew a line through the air.

"You have the ability to kill, justly, and not let it eat at you." I looked down at my hands. I struggled with all the people who had died so far in this war. And I knew many more would, maybe even people I knew and loved. "You can live in the moment. I can't."

She reached out and clutched my hand. "It's OK, Bran. We will keep the innocent safe, or we'll try, anyway."

I sighed. "I know. It's just that people are more complicated, and good and evil isn't always black and white. Some of those that died back at the lab were only there because Eagle was using a loved one to control them. They were still innocents in a way. I'll never be able to let that go, even if I didn't pull a trigger or slit a throat."

"They died to protect someone they loved. Don't forget that. They did a righteous thing. I'm also sorry they were killed, but if we dwell on it, we won't be able to function or win. This is war, and in war, not all the innocents survive. We'll use our best judgment; that's all we can do."

I nodded. I knew this in my head, but my heart was hurt. I changed the subject. "What's the difference between a weasel and a ferret?"

She looked at me. I wasn't as familiar with the animal kingdom as Piper. She'd spent many years out and about in the wilderness, running into every creature there was. And I was truly curious. The pictures I'd seen made them look about the same—cute, long, furry animals.

Her eyes narrowed. "Ferrets are pets. Weasels are killers to the core."

"What?" I wasn't expecting that answer.

"Weasels will kill larger prey than themselves. They do it brutally, usually going for the throat or the neck and not letting up until they've chewed into something vital, and the other animal is dead. They'll do it for sport as well. They are not an animal to mess with." She shuddered.

"But they're small," I whined. That I did know. Weasels weren't a big animal like the werewolves or even a normal wolf. They were tiny in comparison.

She shrugged. "No one told *them* that."

Well, that didn't help my anxiety. That woman was hunting me. I guess woman wasn't the correct descriptor. God? Or more likely, demon? That felt closer to the truth. She hadn't done anything to me yet but offer intimidation and to let me know she was stalking me. "Do weasels stalk their prey? Do they hunt in packs?" That was a terrifying thought.

She cocked her head. "Yes, they stalk their prey. Usually from a well-hidden piece of brush. They hunt whatever they want, but they are smart about it. No, they don't hunt in packs. They are solitary. They only come together to breed, like some of the wild cats."

Maybe that explained some of Weasel's behavior, especially her breakup with Raven and her subsequent hookup with his brother. It explained her solitary stalking of me. It might even explain what she was going to do to me next—bite my neck and kill me. My hand lifted involuntarily to cover and protect my throat.

Piper's eyebrows scrunched together. "What are you doing?"

"Picturing Weasel trying to rip my throat out."

"Good grief, Bran, she'll probably have a minion do that." Then she smirked.

I punched her in the arm. "That's not funny. She is stalking me."

The mirth left her face. "I know, sorry. It was just too heavy in here."

A tremble entered my voice. "She's after me, I know it." I cleared my throat, trying to make my voice strong again. "I don't know why, though. Maybe because I'm the weakest link?"

Piper scoffed. "She's an idiot if she thinks that. You may be the weakest physically, but she doesn't know what you can do."

"What can I do? Freeze her hand? Burn her hair off? Give her a shock? That's nothing to her!" The panic was building again. Some of it a warning from my magic, some just plain old fear. Being shot had done something to me. I wasn't as brave as I had been.

My throat stopped up, and I couldn't breathe. I could feel myself falling backward. I had no control over it. Then everything went black.

Chapter 3

I woke up laying on the hard floor of Piper's new kitchen. The ceiling was nice. It was bright white and looked like a perfect paint job. There was a cushion under my head when I reached behind me. It was my brown leather jacket. I'd had it slung over the back of the kitchen chair before I... "What happened?" I asked.

Piper was sitting cross legged next to me. "You had a vision."

I struggled up to a sitting position. I brushed my hair back. "What did I say?"

She looked hesitant. She was afraid to answer. I saw her struggle with herself, but then the tension left her shoulders as she decided to tell me. "Well..."

Fletcher walked in. "What are you two doing on the floor?" he asked, and then opened the fridge and pulled out a can of something. I couldn't tell what it was from my position.

Piper looked at me. "Bran had a vision."

Fletcher looked slightly alarmed, then he sat at the table and waited. She sighed.

"So, you gave us another warning about Weasel. I got that from your tone, but the vision was one of those allegorical ones, so I'm not sure what it means, *exactly*." She stood and pulled me up. I grabbed my jacket, put it back on the chair, and sat.

"So, what was it?" I asked impatiently.

"Well, it started with a weasel hiding in the forest, under the grass."

"That sounds pretty straight forward," I said, more snottily than I intended.

Piper ignored me and continued. "A caribou walks by, and the weasel watches but does nothing. Then a wolf goes by, and the same thing. Basically, a parade of animals goes by, and weasel doesn't react. Finally, a black cat walks by, and the weasel leaps in front of it and screams, then the cat morphs into a Bean Sidhe. They fight for a long time, and both are wounded grievously, but the rest of the animals that had walked by come back and join the fight. The weasel is losing, then a giant eagle comes in and snatches up the weasel and flies off. Then you woke up."

I thought for a moment. It didn't seem that hard to interpret, but some things were strange. "The weasel is obviously Weasel, and she's waiting for something to happen. The eagle is obviously Eagle. Are we assuming the black cat is me? If so, why a cat? I'm not a shifter. Also, if the cat is me, why do I morph into a Bean Sidhe? Why is Weasel waiting for me?"

She shrugged. "Yup. That was my take. So again, I'm not sure what it means."

My visions could be so nerve wracking. On one hand, they'd helped us in the past, giving warnings, so to speak, or explanations. This one was more of a mystery than a solution. It increased my stress about being stalked rather than helping me. It must have shown on my face.

Piper looked alarmed. "Are you OK?"

Fletcher handed me a glass of water. I drank several large gulps, then pushed it away. I looked over the table. Fletcher was drinking some form of beer in a can, but I didn't recognize the brand. "Do you have another one of those?" I asked and pointed at the can. He didn't answer, just got up and retrieved one from the fridge. Piper drew her brows together. The hardest thing I usually drank was the occasional glass of wine. I never drank beer. But I needed something to calm my nerves.

I popped the top and drank. Nasty stuff, beer. But I gagged it down. "I don't know what to do." My hair fell forward over my face as I leaned over the table, head in my hands. The panic was building again. Why was I like this?

Piper put her arm around me. "Breathe, Bran." She wasn't a touchy-feely person, so she must have been worried.

I realized I was panting, hyperventilating. So, I slowed my breathing down to large slow breaths and tried to get a handle on my growing panic.

"We don't even know if you are the cat in the vision. There isn't any reason to get worked up over nothing. This could be about something else entirely and may not even be you. Besides, if it is, it shows you give as well as you get in the fight, and Weasel is either killed and eaten by Eagle or rescued by him. So, win win."

I laughed, which was her point. It was almost impossible to panic if you were laughing. "Thanks." I could feel myself blush. "Since getting shot, I've...not been myself."

She frowned. "Of course not. That was huge. No one expects you to be normal. Don't be so hard on yourself."

I nodded. It still didn't help. I was ashamed at reacting like this. At allowing Weasel to frighten and intimidate me. I gathered my wits and courage. I pushed the beer away and looked at Fletcher apologetically. "Thanks for this."

He nodded. "If you want, we can arrange to have someone with you at all times." He looked at Piper, who nodded. "We can work in shifts."

I shook my head. "I can't let you do that. It's too much."

Piper looked at me with a twinkle in her eye. "I'm sure Fred would do it."

"Stop, Pipe. Just stop."

She laughed. Fletcher put up his hands in the universal, "do not involve me in this" sign.

We all fell serious again.

"I think we need to do it. I'll put out the word, and we'll put together a team to keep you safe," Fletcher said.

Piper nodded along.

I wanted to wave it away, but the relief of having someone with me was too much. I nodded.

"It's done," he said, and took out his phone. He texted a few words and put his phone away.

"Are you doing OK staying at your parent's?" Piper asked.

I'd been afraid of leading people to them but hadn't had much of a choice since my friends were also without a place to stay for a while. I didn't trust myself to speak, so I shook my head, no.

"You'll come stay with us until you get your own place," Piper said, and Fletcher nodded. I watched their body language for any hesitation. I didn't see any. They were a new couple basically, and I doubted they wanted company in their first place together. I knew Piper would always take me in, we were closer than sisters, but Fletcher may not want someone homing in on his territory. A wave of gratitude washed through me.

"Thanks."

"You can stay tonight, but there's no furniture. If you want to come back tomorrow, I'll make sure there's a bed at least," Fletcher said.

I nodded. "Thanks." It seemed to be the only thing I could say. I took another drink of my water. "I'll come back tomorrow. I have something I have to do tonight, and I'll need to get my stuff anyway, so tomorrow is soon enough. Thanks so much. I love you both."

Fletcher hugged me when I got up. Werewolves were more physical than normal people, I observed. Piper was usually not into casual hugging, and I certainly wasn't. But it was nice to feel protected, something wolves were good at. Just being here made me feel safe. But I had to go back to work to close and get fixed up for my date with Jed. Something I'd managed to forget for a minute. I said goodbye and left.

The girl working looked at me a little strangely when I got back to the store. I didn't think anything of it until I went into the bathroom and saw my face. My mascara was smudged under my eyes, and my hair was a tangled mess. It looked like I'd been sleeping in my car for days. My employee must have thought I was either out having a tumble in the sheets with someone or day drinking. I sighed.

I fixed my face, renewed my mascara, brushed my hair, and tamed it down. I tended to twist it up in a messy bun when I was working, but since I was going out tonight, I wore it down. My eyes were a little red from my emotional melt down, but it brought out the blue. I shrugged; they'd clear up before tonight. I had on a dark purple "Lunatic Fringe" t-shirt, which was the store's work uniform, and I wore my short, dark brown leather jacket and jeans. I wasn't dressed up. The Bear's Tooth was a casual date night place. You sat in the theater, and they brought you the food you ordered beforehand. Mostly pizza, but you could get other things.

I went up front and told my employee, Amanda, she could go. It was only an hour until closing, so I wouldn't be alone for long, and Jed would be by at seven, anyway. I pushed my rising panic down at being alone. I needed to get over this and soon, or I'd be worthless when everyone needed me.

Before she left, Amanda told me we'd only had a handful of customers. I thanked her and took her seat up front. I was pondering how I was going to deal with Jed when the bell over the door tinkled and a customer walked in. I looked up. Not a customer, Fred.

Chapter 4

A small mix of panic and relief ran through me. Relief because it was Fred, and I'd never felt safer with anyone else. Panic because Jed was picking me up, and I still wasn't sure where I stood with Fred or if he knew Jed was pursuing me. He had to, though. Jed was flirty and open when he was around me. It was obvious he was interested.

I stood up. "Hi," I said in surprise.

He looked a little uncomfortable. But he threw me a panty dropping smile, and my knees nearly buckled. His voice rumbled. "How are you doing?"

With him it wasn't the start of small talk. He was seriously asking me how I was doing, and I knew that from the intensity of his gaze. He looked me over as though checking for wounds. I had them, but the wounds were mental, not physical anymore.

"I'm mostly healed, on the outside," I answered truthfully. I doubted I could lie in his presence without his knowledge.

"That is…good." His normal stoic face held a small frown.

"Why are you here?" I asked. "Sorry, that sounded rude. I'm just curious. Are you shopping?"

"No." His body language relaxed, and he casually shoved his hands into the pockets of his jeans. "I'm your bodyguard."

I laughed, but he didn't join in. I knew he was serious. "Bodyguard? I asked for help, but nothing that intrusive. I just thought I'd get a bird shifter checking in on me."

"This is better. No one will get through me."

I believed that. And I felt safe with him. Now I had to tell him I was going on a date with Jed, or that would get awkward fast.

"Um," I looked up to the left, an unfortunate tell that I was uncomfortable. "I only need someone until seven."

He looked at me sharply. "Is that when you travel to your parent's home?"

I shook my head. "No, it's when I close the store, but I have a date tonight."

"I am aware."

My eyes opened wide. "How? I've only told Piper?" She told on me, my *best* friend.

"Jed told me."

That sent a shock through me. Why would he do that? Was it some kind of male posturing? Was he giving Fred a "stay out of my territory" threat?

"What?" I asked stupidly.

"I will be accompanying you both."

"On a date?" My mouth must have been hanging open or something stupid because I couldn't get my head around this situation. "Isn't that weird? I mean…" I made a back-and-forth motion with my hands to indicate the connection between us.

"I'm not thrilled, either."

"I'm just going to cancel. This was a stupid idea, anyway." I sighed.

"That would not be fair to Jed."

When I was nervous, I tended to blurt out whatever I was thinking. Damn the torpedoes, etc. "I'm not attracted to Jed. I thought it would be better for me to be…that way, but it didn't work. I'm just going to hurt both of us. It would be better to just call it off for good."

"Call what off?" A voice rang out even before the bell over the door stopped jingling.

Jed was dressed casually, but nice. His jeans looked new, and he had on a fitted long-sleeved t-shirt, a denim jacket, and too much cologne, which if I could tell from here, must be obnoxious to Fred and himself. I hoped it faded before we ate.

"Nothing important," I answered. I threw a brief glance at Fred and saw the moment we both resigned ourselves to the night ahead. I promised myself that this would be a one and done, and after tonight, I'd let Jed down easily.

I looked up at the clock. It was ten minutes to seven. I figured I might as well close, there weren't any customers and the sooner the three of us left, the sooner this disaster would be closer to over. I sighed. I balanced out the till and put up the closed sign. The men walked out, then I locked the door behind the three of us. I had a moment where I wondered what would happen if I just locked myself in and avoided the whole thing, but it passed before anyone noticed.

My red crossover was in the parking lot as was Jed's older Subaru Outback. Fred looked at both and shook his head. "I'll drive."

Neither of us replied; we just walked to Fred's huge SUV.

"Is this thing armored?" I asked snarkily as I climbed in the front seat.

"Yes," he replied simply.

I wasn't really expecting that answer, but it explained why he wanted to drive. "Oh."

He started the engine. My store wasn't that far away from the Bear's Tooth, but we had to navigate a few lights and some traffic. Plus, the Bear's Tooth was always busy. It was a popular place, and I knew parking would be a beast, especially in this monstrosity. Not my problem, I started chanting under my breath.

"Is something wrong?" Fred asked.

I forgot for a moment to keep all sounds to myself—werewolf. That meant Jed probably heard me too, but I had no idea what swan hearing was like. With my luck, fantastic. "No, everything's perfect, why do you ask?"

He didn't answer, and no one jumped into the conversation in the back, so swan hearing mustn't be as good as wolf.

We turned down the road to the Bear's Tooth. Cars lined both sides of the street and filled the parking lot in front. The parking lot to the side was also full, but a giant truck backed out of a space just as Fred pulled up. Darn my luck.

We clambered out, Jed came around to help me, and Fred stood and watched, his jaw clenched.

"Thanks," I mumbled.

Jed already had the tickets, so we skipped the ticket line and went inside. People were standing in line even though it was still forty-five minutes to showtime. Fred agreed to hold the place in line, so we took his food request and went up to order. We had to wait a bit to place our orders, but we made it up to the window soon enough. Jed insisted on paying. I argued, since I didn't want him to bear the burden of three meals, especially two of those being shifter sized meals. I was also feeling guilty about the whole situation. He was a poor college student; I was a somewhat successful businesswoman. It didn't make sense. But he won, and he paid. We took our drinks, the number for our table, and went back to stand in line with Fred.

Fred wasn't good at small talk. At all. You'd think after living for so long, he'd be a master. This was probably a choice. After all that time he must be seriously tired of other people and their crap. Jed at least had the stuff down. He kept us both entertained with his tales—all fluff, but at least neither Fred nor I had to say much more than, "cool, really, that's nice," and other ridiculous things.

My mind could wander since there wasn't much to pay attention to. I could coo and coddle without engaging my mind. I put that part of me on autopilot and started reaching out with my senses, just in case. I had a tendency to let my guard down around Fred, but I'd been trying to force myself to be more aware of my surroundings. I thought I caught a flicker of power. But I was next to Jed.

I searched some more, but it was gone. I must have just caught Jed's signature and when I focused, it was there, steady and true, if weak. Fred, as always, was a blank on the magical spectrum. I furrowed my brow. Huh, I could almost track him that way. Everyone, human, or magical, gave off some type of feeling. Life had a feeling.

Fred was a black hole. I wondered how long it had taken him to perfect a shield so absolute. I focused back on the conversation a few moments after I realized they were waiting for my reply.

"Oh, sorry, I was woolgathering. What did you ask?" I blinked.

"Sorry, I asked if you'd heard good things about the movie," Jed answered.

"Yeah, it's supposed to be good. I'm excited to see it." I tried to add some pep to my voice. Jed's expression seemed to light up, so I must have hit the right note. I didn't really care about the movie either way. I didn't even know what it was. I looked down at my ticket. The blood drained from my face. I let my hair fall forward to disguise it. I groaned, involuntarily.

Fred's eyes flicked to me.

I was hoping for a big action flick, something benign or exciting, but it wasn't. It was a love story. I closed my eyes. A string of curses filled my mind—I may not say them, but I knew them. I looked at both men, judging their reactions under my lashes.

Jed was still smiling at me. I wanted to pound my head into a wall. I'd said I was excited to see the movie, he must have read into that. Just my luck. It was rated "R" as well, that meant at least one sex scene, probably more. I looked for the exits. One was the door we'd entered through. The others must be down by the screen inside the theater we were waiting outside of. Fred was aloof. I'd offended him too. I was about to sit in a dark theater with two men that were interested in me. Why hadn't I locked myself in my store?

Since I couldn't flee, I resigned myself to my fate—the most awkward night ever. I sighed and tried to focus back on the conversation before I unwittingly added more fuel to Jed's fire.

Again, although I wasn't searching, I felt a strong twinge of magic. I frowned and looked around. Fred immediately became alert.

"What's wrong?" he asked, his voice deep and rough.

"I thought I felt a strong magic signature. Twice." I shook my head. "It's gone, again. I'm probably just picking up people moving around outside."

Fred looked like he wanted to shift and search the area. It was subtle, but I picked up on him scenting for anything foreign. I had no idea how strong a wolf's nose was, but with all the food smells and people smells, and Jed's cologne, I didn't know what he thought he'd pick up. I didn't say anything. It was probably his instinct to try.

"I'm going to the bathroom," Fred said abruptly.

Jed and I nodded.

I knew he was going to search for whatever I'd sensed.

He wandered off, and I turned my attention to my date. Just in time for him to try to put his arm around me. I acted like my shoe was untied, and I ducked down to tie it before he completed the gesture. Then to further hide my act, I said, "I want to apologize. I didn't intend to have a second man on our date."

Jed recovered and chuckled. "Yeah, me either."

"Did he tell you why?"

"No, but Piper did. She called me and said Fletcher asked him to watch over you for a while until she could set up a proper schedule with the other shifters. She told me about your vision."

I nodded. Jed understood. One of my visions had probably saved his life.

"Fred said you told him about our date tonight."

"Yeah, I was hoping he'd take the hint that I'd take care of you, and he wouldn't have to. But he just nodded. Then, he obviously showed up."

"Sorry."

"It's OK. Better safe than sorry. We both know in a fight, we want Fred. I just figured I could handle stuff in a crowded theater. Who would attack us here?"

Famous last words. I felt a shiver of primal fear, not a full premonition, but a dark surety that something bad was about to happen. I was looking into Jed's grey eyes, his face confused at the expression on my face just as the screaming started.

Jed, bless his heart, jumped in front of me. I scanned desperately for the source of the screams. There were so many people, and I was at the low end of average height. I couldn't see anything, but I could feel the curiosity and fear build in the crowd. I shut down my overwhelmed magical senses. Where was Fred? Did he really just go to the bathroom? Was the attack planned for the second he left? My heart was pounding in my chest, and I felt slightly faint.

Then I saw it. I think when I thought about weasels, I pictured a cute little animal like a pet ferret. I knew they were nasty and mean, Piper had said so, but that's what I had in mind. I kept forgetting that most of the truly old shifters like Fred had forms from the time of the ice age and earlier—megafauna. This weasel was taller at the shoulder than a lynx. It was long and could be roughly identified as a weasel, I guess. Nothing about it was cute. I bet it weighed a hundred and twenty to a hundred and fifty pounds. Its jaws and teeth looked like a nightmare. There was nothing that looked like it was from this day and age, and it was utterly terrifying.

"*Megalictis ferox.*" A voice whispered in my ear, I jumped and fell into Fred.

"What?"

"Giant wolverine, a misnomer. It's a weasel."

"Who cares! I can see it. What do we do? It wants me."

He growled, and it rattled my bones. The weasel was tossing people aside quickly, and we didn't have much time. Staying here was going to get people hurt or killed. Fred grabbed my arm and started pulling me through the crowd towards the theater doors. The people inside watching the end of the movie were completely unaware of the horror outside. Those that had been waiting in line with us were also trying to push into the theater to get to the other exit since the giant weasel was between them and the main doors.

"Why would she attack here?" I asked, but Fred was too busy trying to get me out that he didn't answer. My mind was working overtime, trying to keep my growing panic down. I had no idea where Jed was. He was vulnerable. The enemy had it out for him, and he was a shifter, sure, but a swan. Swans were formidable, and they had a tendency to take on creatures larger than themselves once their temper was up, but he wasn't any match for that monster. I hoped he got out. I liked him—I wanted him to stay alive.

Fred continued to pull me through the crowds. We bumped into people, and I stumbled many times. His size and ferocity got through even the panicked crowd. Finally, we were near the exit by the screen. I didn't want to use my physical shield. It would help us move the crowd aside, but it would shut down everyone's electronics and they might need them. I looked behind us; Weasel was coming. I threw up the shield anyway, and the crowd parted around us. Fred pushed us through the last of the crowd, and we stumbled out into the side parking lot.

I kept trying to figure out why now? She'd had chances in much less crowded places. Did she want to expose shifters? Did she care? How did she even find out where I was? I was careful to not follow a routine except when I was at my store. She could have gone there and done this in quiet. No, she had some reason. I just didn't know what it was.

Once we stumbled out into the night and cleared the crowd, three bear shifters faced us in their animal form. One was a polar bear. I remember hearing the others talk about Nanuq. That meant this bear was as old as Fred. Nearly immortal. This was it. Even Fred couldn't take on this. The shadow winged ones, no problem, my money was on Fred. But between Weasel and Nanuq? We were seriously screwed.

We stopped in front of them as people, screaming and crying, streamed past us—taking a wide berth around the bears. I could hear sirens. I didn't know what the police were going to do, but they didn't know their bullets and handcuffs were worthless. Maybe high-powered tranquilizers? I doubt they carried those around. The stream of people and cars leaving in a panic were going to keep them from the action for several minutes though.

The giant weasel burst through the exit door. Her fur was coated with blood and gore. She was behind us. Fred turned so his body was bladed, and he could keep the bears and the weasel in his sight. Weasel shifted, and the beautiful Malina stood in her naked, if bloody, glory. She would have made my namesake look plain. Even in my fear, I felt a twinge of jealousy until I realized she could choose her form.

I gathered my courage. "What do you want?"

Fred's growl rattled my bones, and I wondered if he would shift.

She took a few steps closer. Even covered in blood and gore, she exuded charm and sex with every step, using her body—the curve of her breasts, the sway of her hips, to keep everyone's attention. I was horrified, but still I could see how both Raven and Eagle had been enamored of her. In a flash of insight, I realized this was part of her magic, and instantly her pull ended, and I sneered at her.

She stopped inches from me, reached out her hand, and brushed my hair gently away from my face.

"I have need of you, little witch," her voice caressed and seduced.

"I don't swing that way," I said with as much contempt as I could muster.

She laughed throatily and looked me up and down. I grew even more terrified.

"You are a cheeky thing. I have no need of lover. I have another use for you."

Sweat trickled from under my hair, and down my back. "What?"

But she didn't answer, she gestured to the bears, and they grabbed for Fred. He turned and fought. Somewhere in there, he shifted into his half form. I'd only seen it once, and he'd told us it was something he'd discovered recently, but it gave him an advantage. I clutched my hand to my throat; the fight was brutal. Fred ripped through one of the shadow winged shifters, and the bear dropped dead to the ground, its spine ripped out partially from the back of its neck.

Instead of slowing with the death of one of the combatants, the fight amped up. The two remaining bears were forcing Fred back, away from me. He was covered in blood, gouges, and in some places, chunks of flesh were missing. I couldn't stand it. They were going to kill him. Together, they were just too much for even his great heart.

"Stop," I said.

Nothing happened. The sirens were growing louder.

I turned to Weasel. "I'll go with you willingly, just stop them."

She quirked a single eyebrow at me. "Very well, but aren't you enjoying the fun?"

"No."

"OK, boys. Wrap up your fun. We're leaving."

The shadow winged shifter backed off, but Fred didn't stop. Nanuq shifted into a half form like Fred and actually grew in size. The polar werebear stood on two massive paws—a white furred monstrosity. Then to my horror, he swatted Fred. The bear's mass and immense strength sent Fred flying ten feet or more. He skidded and lay still. I gasped. Was he dead? I watched; his ribcage moved. He was alive, just out cold. I turned to Weasel. "Leave him be, and I won't give you any trouble."

She scanned my face, judging my honesty. She must have been satisfied because she called off the polar bear, who shifted back into a man. They walked over to a large SUV, not unlike Fred's, and casually dressed. Now, they were just people fleeing a scary situation at a local theater.

Maybe Weasel would even get away with it. Especially since humans loved to spin anything supernatural into something mundane. I imagined the news would be full of tales of escaped zoo animals or some such rubbish. I don't know how they'd explain the huge pre-ice-age weasel, but I'm sure it would become a big cat in the news report.

I got into the vehicle. Fred's body had morphed back to human, something he could only do if he was alive. I breathed another sigh of relief at that assurance, then I leaned back in the seat to meet my fate.

Chapter 5

Now that I knew Fred was safe, I worried about Jed. Had he made it out alive? Uninjured? I had no way to know. I felt the guilt build again. If I'd called off this sham of a date, he'd be safe at home. I may not want to date him, but I wished him no ill. We drove out of Midtown and headed south.

Since I had nothing to lose—they didn't seem to want me dead—I asked, "Why aren't you blindfolding me or something?"

Weasel laughed. "You watch too many movies. You already know where we are going, so what's the point?"

I did? I only knew of two Eagle locations, and only one of those was in Southtown. We must be heading back to the lab where Piper and Raven had freed a bunch of shifters from certain death. I shivered. Is that what they were going to do to me? Cut me up and use my parts in a new type of Frankensteinian monster? I felt ill. If they were taking me to the lab, wouldn't that make it easier for my people to find me? Were they planning on that, setting another trap?

My hands were shaking. Probably shock, I thought calmly. Maybe I'd die of that and not have to face whatever they were planning to do with me. By now, Fred would have healed from his wounds and found

Jed. I hope they avoided the police. That's all I could do for them. Hope. I sent a silent prayer, too.

I looked at Weasel. Or at least the back of her head. She sat in the passenger seat, one of her minions driving, the other next to me, keeping an eye out. I didn't know much about weasels. Raven always said the Sky People took on the characteristics of their animal totem. I probably should have spent more time researching actual weasels than trying to find Weasel folklore. Idiot. What I learned from Piper was that weasels were great hunters. I thought she'd said they were loners though. If so, why was she allied with Eagle? Were they still together? After hearing the stories Raven told about her, I doubted she'd stayed with Eagle much longer than she'd stayed with Raven. I shook my head. I wasn't sure, and I doubted any of what I knew would help me.

I had to stick with the facts. I was alone. I was overpowered, and I was at the mercy of Weasel and her bears. I had no idea how long it would take my friends to find me at the lab. It was so obvious, that I bet it was the last place they'd think of. Apparently, Weasels were thinkers, planners, and evil geniuses. Add that to your list, Wiki. I sighed.

I could try to escape. I had my zapper. That could give me up to fifteen seconds. At least it had when I'd used it on a supernatural before. I could leap out of the car and run to freedom. I'd have to time it close to a stoplight. We were on the highway right now. I looked around. I must have given myself away, because Nanuq, who was sitting next to me said, "The doors are locked. You can't get free."

I tried the door latch anyway. Nothing happened. Maybe I could pop the lock with magic. I concentrated on it. I didn't understand how the mechanism worked, so I couldn't deactivate the lock.

Maybe I could try something when we stopped, and they took me out of the car. Hope blazed up. I glared at the polar werebear. He winked at me, and gave me the slow once over look of the sexual predator, rather than the killer. I shivered. For a moment, I wondered if he had been one of the bears that had defiled my home. I could handle dying by being torn apart from teeth and claws. I did not want to be raped.

I turned back to the window. Silent tears ran down my face. More from frustration than fear, I told myself. We turned on the Dimond exit, and then another turn onto Old Seward. We drove a few blocks to a familiar building. The SUV pulled around to the warehouse entrance and into one of the bays. I sat up straighter and readied my magic.

The vehicle stopped, and the driver turned off the engine. Doors opened. Nanuq, came around and opened my door and pulled me out roughly. I stumbled and nearly fell. He yanked me up. I placed my hands on him and gave him the biggest zap I could manage. That zap had laid out *weres* before. Nanuq grunted, his muscles tensed, and I could tell I'd hurt him, but he didn't fall. Instead, he slapped me across the face and knocked me to the ground.

The slap must have knocked my brain around pretty good, because it took me a minute to figure out what happened. When I did, I was being yanked back to my feet. I reached up to feel my face. My cheek was bleeding. He'd hit me *hard*. Still, he must have been careful because I had no doubt, he could kill me with a single swat. My face throbbed, and my head was muzzy. His grip on my arm was like iron, and I knew that between him and Fred, I would be covered with bruises down both arms tomorrow. At least Fred had been trying to save me. I'd cherish *those* bruises.

My lip turned up involuntarily. My face must be swelling fast. I reached up with my free hand to check, yup. I glared at the werebear and thought of ways I could hurt him. My zapper was my best defense and that hadn't done much but anger him. That left me with just the freeze or the heat ray. Since the zapper didn't do anything, I bet he'd laugh at the other two tricks I had, ice probably would just tickle a polar bear. If I could concentrate long enough, I could probably cook his testicles. I stared at them, forcing my heat ray to do just that, but he yanked me forward again, and I lost my concentration.

The werebear continued to drag me after Weasel. She exited through a door next to the roll-up door and walked around to the front of the building. We entered. The building was beautiful and looked like big money. All glass, marble, and expensive wood. I was pulled past the desk and down a corridor to the elevators. I chuckled nervously. I remembered my vision about the lazy doctor complaining about walking down six flights of stairs. They must have fixed the elevator.

Sure enough, Weasel pressed the level for sub-basement six. The secret lab of horrors. I gulped and my knees buckled. The werebear jerked me back up. I folded in the middle and threw up all over his shoes. He threw me back into the wall of the elevator in disgust.

Weasel looked at him coldly. "Please don't damage the merchandise."

He shook off his shoe. At least my stomach had been mostly empty, we hadn't eaten before the attack. He looked murderous though. If Weasel weren't here, I'd be dead. I did not want to feel gratitude towards her. That's how Stockholm Syndrome started—I couldn't forget that these people were evil incarnate.

The doors slid open soundlessly, and we faced a corridor with a door at the end. We stepped out, and they pulled me to the door. Weasel waved a card in front of a reader, and the door clicked open. The bear pulled me down another corridor, this one lined with doors. It was quiet—no one else was around. That was eerie. I looked for help from anywhere, but I knew I shouldn't get my hopes up. Where were my friends? Would they find me?

Weasel finally stopped in front of a door. She swiped her card, and it opened. Nanuq pulled me in through one room and into an operating theater of some kind. Yep, they were gonna cut me up into Bran chunks. I wasn't a shifter though. Were they gonna feed me to their patchwork monsters?

Once Weasel stopped and moved out of my view, I noticed that this operating theater was missing a component besides compassion. A bed. Instead, the space was taken up by a gigantic, black, metal coffin. I tried to back away. I knew what it was. The artifact. But this was impossible. My side still had the gold.

"No, how can this be?"

Weasel grinned. "I'm so glad you asked. You obviously know what this is?"

I nodded weakly, resigned.

"You don't have the gold," I repeated, only this time out loud.

"It's just gold. However, we discovered we need the gold your raven friend has for the artifact to run properly. You see, there isn't enough magic for it to work without your gold. Apparently, it contained something we can't…replicate." She waved her hand as she thought of the word.

"The poor creatures we attempted to change didn't come out—as they should."

I swallowed my rising bile. "What does that mean?"

"They weren't…viable."

"It killed them?" My voice was hitting whine level.

"You could say that. Let's just say, they are happier dead."

I shuddered, and my knees wobbled. The werebear jerked me up to standing again.

"So, I had a great idea. We could use a human witch. The power would be there for the extra boost. And the best part of my idea is I knew where to find one. They aren't as plentiful as they used to be, you know."

"No, I didn't." I said under my breath, but Weasel heard me and laughed.

"Oh yes, the place used to be crawling with them. They are a little more wary about showing who they are now, so I can't always locate one. But then this bright little pulse of power kept showing up when I went past a silly little shop in Midtown. At first, I was sure it was Raven's daughter. You can imagine my surprise to see a pale, *human* woman. But the power signature was just yummy. And here we are! Everything is working out as it should. You might even call it providence."

"I wouldn't."

"Well, you should. This will be a grand adventure, if you survive."

"What are you going to do to me?"

"You know what I'm going to do. You'll go in my lovely machine." She swept a hand over it lovingly. "And you'll come out twisted, dead, or a *were*. I'm hoping for the last of course. I like your spirit."

"What kind of *were*? A wolf?" The pitch of my voice went up in my terror.

"Is that what you hope? Your wolf didn't tell you how it worked?" she asked.

I couldn't get in a deep breath. I didn't want to change. I was me; I didn't know how to be different. Also, there was no guarantee this would work. It hadn't yet, this was Weasel experimenting with my life for her entertainment.

I gulped in another gasp of air and choked out, "No, well, only generally. I have no idea otherwise."

Weasel casually folded her arms like we were having a pleasant conversation.

"This is the best part of the magic. We can program some things, but the truth is, even those of us that have used it and even helped build it aren't always sure of the results. See, the machine picks out the animal, predator, that you most closely align yourself with. In a way, the creature that most closely resembles your spirit. I'm betting you're going to come out as a type of cat. Curious, prickly, and will fight when cornered. We took bets."

A cat? I wasn't a predator at all. I barely liked to eat meat. I hated violence. I'd even turn spiders out of my house rather than smash them. And I hated spiders. I don't know why I worried. I was probably gonna die in that thing. If I was a cat, how would Fred feel? He hated cats. Every time we brought them up, he talked about how untrustworthy they were. Why was that what I was thinking right now? I focused back on the moment.

"Any other questions? It's the least we can do before we start. We want you to be comfortable." She reached up to smooth her hair and came back with a piece of gore. She frowned at her hand and flicked the bloody piece of flesh to the floor.

"No, you don't. You're doing this against my will. You don't care at all."

I stared at the artifact. It gave off a malevolent feel. I wasn't sure if that was real, or my interpretation of the situation. I reached out with my magic, just a thread. I didn't know if my magic was even compatible with the thing. Raven had said you needed the blood of the Sky People in you to operate it. I guess I wasn't operating it though. Just providing the juice it was missing from the gold. It sounded like I was just an experiment, anyway. My magic might not work on it, and I'd come out like her other experiments. Broken and dead. But I felt...something. Something alien but curious. Was the artifact sentient? That would be a twist. If it was, I wondered how it liked being in that pond for over a century. Angry. That's what I'd be. I shivered. Would it take its anger out on me? I focused back on the evil diatribe Weasel was spewing.

"You gave us permission. I believe that was your intent when you traded yourself for the wolf?"

Well, that was a conundrum. I had. I'd told her I'd do what she wanted for Fred's life. I straightened my spine. "Yes." I couldn't really answer differently. I had no doubt she'd send the polar werebear back out for him if I failed to carry out her plans. I may not be big magic in this world, but I could protect those I cared about with what I had. In this case, my life.

"Good. Please repeat after me." She waited until I nodded. "I, state your full name, enter of my own free will."

My throat was dry, and when I started to say it, I coughed. Then I stopped. "Promise me, you will not go after Fred or Jed and will not harm them in any way."

She hesitated, but answered, "Yes, I do swear." Her body language was stiff, she was growing impatient.

I nodded. Her answer felt binding. Like a magical oath.

"After I do this, my oath is satisfied," I said firmly, if a little shakily.

She started to look annoyed. Apparently, she'd seen zero need to work on her stoic face like Raven and Fred had.

"Fine, I agree. Now say it." She wasn't going to allow me to stall any longer.

I looked around for a way to escape. Nothing. I swallowed and started again, "I, Branwyn Brigid O'Connor, enter of my own free will."

She clapped her hands together. "Brilliant. Step over here."

I couldn't move, the werebear still had my arm in his vice grip. He was holding me so tight my lower arm and hand were numb.

She looked up at the werebear as though she had forgotten him. "You are dismissed."

He growled and took a step forward as though to challenge her, then thought better of it, turned on his heel, and walked out.

I rubbed my arm where he'd clutched it and stepped over to the spot she indicated. "You'll need to strip."

I wrapped my arms around myself. I didn't want this creature to see me naked. It was the last bit of dignity I had. She gave me a moment. Then because I was doing it for Fred and Jed, I stripped. I tried to cover myself with my hands, which was inadequate. I wasn't fat, but I was shapely.

"If you are wearing jewelry, that will have to come off too."

She could have said that first, but I wasn't wearing any. My hair was down, so there wasn't any point in wearing earrings. I didn't usually wear rings, and I hadn't been dressed up enough for bracelets or necklaces. I shook my head.

"Fine. Come around to this side." She walked to the far side.

I could see that the machine was open as I walked around. She indicated how I should enter and which direction I should lie down. I complied.

"This won't be pleasant. I'll see you on the other side." Her voice was cheerful, like I was having an MRI, not a magical DNA change.

I was shaking and sweat poured from every pore. All I could do was watch her close the door. Then, I lay alone in a coffin with soft blue light surrounding me. Since I had to try what I could, I reached out and attempted to communicate with the device.

It wasn't talking. The device was too alien. I tried to impress on it that I didn't wish to change. I focused my will on that one thought, pressing my humanity into its machine mind. The machine was silent. I relaxed. Maybe I'd broken it, or unlike Weasel's speech, it wasn't going to work on me. Maybe I didn't have enough magic to make it run. That wasn't right. A Sky Person or shadow winged had to run it.

My power was going to give it the extra boost the missing magical gold should have provided.

I tried to push the door back open with my hands. I didn't have a lot of space to maneuver, but it didn't matter. I couldn't budge the door. She probably had to release it from the outside. I hadn't noticed any visible latches or controls. I guess they would only show themselves to the operator. I was starting to feel claustrophobic.

My breathing was coming out harshly in the small space. My heart pounded, and I'd already sweated so much that I was sliding around in the rounded hole I was lying in. Nothing happened for a long while. Then I felt a slight hum. I stilled. The blue light intensified. The hard surface I was on began to mold and soften around me until it completely encapsulated me. Every piece of me was covered by the artifact. I felt something enter my nostril, mouth, and other orifices. I couldn't move. I was suffocating. I felt like my heart and lungs would explode in my panic.

The hum continued to build until I realized I wasn't hearing it; I was feeling it in my bones. They were vibrating. The light continued to build from gentle to uncomfortable, and I squeezed my eyes shut. I couldn't do anything. I reached out with my magic and tried to force the machine to bend to my will. The hum became pain. The vibration was so much, I knew my bones would shatter if it continued. I lost the thread of my will, my magic.

The light kept increasing until I couldn't block it with my eyelids. And still it built. Even with the smooth metal down my throat, I was screaming. I screamed until I felt a rupture in my throat. I tried to move, to escape, but I couldn't do either and still the light and hum kept building. Now my bones were shattering, and the pain was... I passed out.

Chapter 6

The door opened. I couldn't move or see. Then a dim light started to glow from the door. I turned my head slowly, afraid the pain would hit again, but other than a mild headache, it was gone. I tried to look at my body, to see if the machine had changed me or turned me into a monster. I couldn't see most of my body because the space inside was so tight, but what I could see looked normal.

"You'll probably be feeling weak and strange, but I'll help you out." Weasel's voice grated on my ears. Everything seemed a lot more sensitive. Even my skin felt the vibration of her voice.

I reached out a hand and grasped the side of the artifact and pulled myself out carefully. I was weak. Shaky, like I hadn't eaten in a while. I moved slowly. I put my feet down and stood. I swayed a little. "What did it do to me?" I asked in a voice that sounded tentative and high.

"We'll know on the next full moon," Weasel said and clapped her hands excitedly.

"Does that mean the artifact worked properly?" I asked, scared that I still might drop dead or be a monster inside.

"You are alive. There's a good chance it worked perfectly! You'll be a wonderful addition to our army."

"What?" I asked stupidly. I knew that was the end game. I just lost sight for a moment. I still needed to get out of here, get away. Where were my friends? "How long was I in there?"

"Hmm, about twelve hours. It varies from person to person. You were surprisingly quick." She was smiling like a child with a new toy, and I was that toy.

I itched. My gunshot wounds itched, I scratched at them. The itching became unbearable. I looked down, and my half-healed wounds began to close before my eyes. I gasped. Once they healed completely, I reached up to my cheek, it was also normal. I looked around for my clothes.

"Where are my clothes?" I asked, suddenly modest as the fog cleared, and I remembered I was naked.

Weasel pointed to a table by the wall, and I staggered to it and dressed. A pain grabbed my middle. I doubled over and groaned. What was that?

"You are hungry. The artifact takes a lot out of you."

I looked down. My jeans were loose, as were the rest of my clothes. I'd dressed so hurriedly, I hadn't noticed. I had lost weight in the last twelve hours. Not the diet plan I would have preferred.

My head snapped up. I thought I heard someone call my name. I reached out with my senses. I could feel them there, just beyond my reach. I tried again. Nothing.

"Where's my magic?" I asked, desperately.

"Well…" Weasel looked away as though she heard someone calling as well. "There's a good possibility you burned it out in the artifact. It may or may not come back. It's a wait and see game." She sighed. Like it mattered to her. "Personally, a *were* with human witch powers would be fascinating. I don't think I've had one before." She cocked her head to one side as though she were imagining all the things she was going to do with me.

I shuddered.

"Bran!"

I definitely heard my name. It wasn't my imagination. Weasel whirled around, a snarl on her face.

The shouting sounded like Piper. Fear, like ice, trickled down my spine. Piper wasn't a match for Weasel and who knew if the two bears or others were still here. Weasel shifted and the ancient creepy weasel form from the theater appeared. She raced through the open doorway and out. I staggered after her, my weakness slowly dissipating, it still felt like my mind wasn't connected to my body, and I had no magic to delay her, not that I could have if I did.

The outer door to the operating suite was shut. It didn't matter. She must have had other powers because it exploded outward before she even touched it. I didn't know what to do.

"Piper, run!" I shouted. My voice was healed I realized, and I employed it with as much volume as I could muster.

I could hear snarling, growling, and snapping up ahead. I skidded to a stop in the now open doorway into the corridor. Weasel, Nanuq, and the shadow winged bear were fighting Piper's Urayuli, Fred's wolf, and what I assumed must be Raven in the same cat form he'd used at Fred's house when we were attacked. A large saber toothed something, not a tiger though.

I was worse than useless. I'd been changed by the artifact into who knew what, but I was currently weak as a kitten. I had no magic, and I might never get it back. All I could do was watch and hope. Raven was surely a match for Weasel. But Fred wasn't a match for Nanuq. I'm sure Piper could take the shadow winged bear, so it was up in the air who would prevail.

The battle was hard to follow, too much movement. Piper's form filled the hallway. It was almost too large to move in the confined space. But her choice was formidable. I couldn't imagine what it would be like to battle a real Urayuli. Maybe she was a real Urayuli. I frowned at the thought. This whole thing was unbelievable.

The smell of blood filled the air and much to my chagrin, my mouth watered. I put my hand over it. *Ooo, yuck,* I thought. What was I?

The fight swung towards my doorway. Without thinking I threw up my shield. A blue light filled the doorway, and a bear bounced off my shield. I blinked in amazement. My magic was still there. I reached for it again. It felt sluggish and dull, but it was starting to respond to me.

Maybe the artifact had drawn from it and drained it, but it was still mine. I breathed a sigh of relief. I couldn't imagine living without it. It was as much a part of me as my arm or my head.

I laughed. My emotions were all over the place. Everything felt strange, new, and I was off balance. I leaned on the doorway. Fred was in his half form, battling the polar werebear. The space was too small for it to use its half form, so he was in his animal form. Fred was losing. My eyes narrowed. She'd promised me no harm would come to him. He was going to die. I could see it as clearly as I could look down and see my hands. Fury erupted throughout my core. I grabbed a hold of every scrap of magic I had, and I reached out and slammed the white bear to the ground and held him there.

I held with all I had. I didn't have much, and my vision was quickly starting to narrow. For a moment more, I could still see the battle. Weasel was a fierce fighter. She looked like she might have the upper hand on Raven's giant cat. She had her teeth sunk into his shoulder where it joined his neck, and he was throwing himself against the wall to squish her or dislodge her.

Piper saw her dad's problem. She screamed and all of us froze.

A primal fear gripped me, and I couldn't move. Even Weasel froze. I lost hold of my magic. Piper used the lull to grab me. She pulled me up in her arms like a baby and ran towards the exit. Still frozen, all I did was lay in her hairy arms. By the time we reached the stairwell, I'd regained my ability to move, so she set me down and morphed back to herself. She threw an oversized t-shirt over her naked body, it had been lying by the stairs, and we both raced up the stairs. Three men were racing down at the same time. I wasn't aware enough to recognize them, but Piper raised a hand as we passed.

"How did you find me?" I puffed as we ran, still tired and weak.

"Fred did. He tracked you."

"How? We were in a car."

"I don't know, you'll have to ask him."

We hit the main floor and raced to the exit. More of our people were piling in. I actually felt safe. Maybe we would prevail. Why hadn't Weasel filled the building with minions? Was she so full of herself, she didn't think my friends would fight back? Was this part of a larger plan? I felt the edge of a premonition begin, but it faded with my dulled magic. I shook my head. I needed to get past this weakness. As we cleared the building and ran for Piper's truck, I heard a boom. Glass shattered all around us. The windows had blown out of the mid-rise Silla Corp. building. We both ducked as glass rained down on us.

I turned. Most of the windows were gone. But the building was still standing. What could have caused that? Then I saw Weasel in her animal form race out, followed by Nanuq. She shifted mid stride, and a hawk rose from the ground and raced off to the south. Nanuq chuffed in frustration. He headed for a copse of trees between the row of buildings on the road and the next street over. Piper grabbed my hand and pulled me to the truck.

Our allies were pouring out of the building. Most back in human form, or still in human form. I saw Fred. His huge wolf bounded towards us, fury shining bright in his eyes. Fletcher was a bright spot behind him. Before I could get the passenger door open, they both leapt into the bed of Piper's truck, and the whole vehicle rocked. Then we were in, heading north—away from Weasel.

"Is your dad, OK?" I asked Piper as she drove.

"Don't know. Probably." Her body language was stiff, tense. She kept looking into the rearview mirror for pursuit, I was sure.

"Where are we going?"

"New place."

She obviously wasn't feeling up to conversations. Once we were a few blocks down the road, she finally relaxed visibly. "Are you OK?"

I was silent. I wasn't sure how to answer that. I didn't know what I was or what had really been done to change me. "I don't know."

"What did they do?"

"They put me in the artifact. She was trying to change me into a *were*."

She paused, the shock showing in her body language. Then a tentative, "Did it work?"

"I don't know. I feel weird, but I appear to be myself. She said I'd know if it was successful on the full moon." My voice was shaky.

"I'm sorry, Bran."

I shrugged. So far, I seemed unaffected. Maybe I'd stay that way. Facing Weasel like I had seemed to cool some of the fear I had of her. I guess time would tell what my new life would be like. "She will keep coming for me. She thinks I'm her property now. I'm supposed to join her army."

"What?" Piper said, alarmed.

"That's what she said. I don't know what it means. I'm no fighter. I'm definitely not keen on being someone's slave." I faced her. "Thank you. I couldn't live like that."

"You need to thank Fred. I would do anything to get you back, but he was berserk. He... Let's just say I think his feelings for you are real."

A feeling, I'm not sure what it was, maybe a cross between elation and dread, filled my heart. I sobbed. I don't even know where that came from, but I was suddenly crying like my heart was forever broken. Piper looked alarmed. I could feel Fred pounding on the window between the front and back of the truck. I glanced his way. He was human, and although his torso was bare, he had on stretchy athletic shorts. His eyes were still shining with emotion, and he looked like he was going to come through the back window. I raised a hand to him to indicate I was alright; he settled down again. But he watched me. I turned back to Piper.

I didn't want Fred to hear me. I turned on the radio, then flipped it to high, and scooted close to Piper. "Weasel seems to think I'm going to be a cat *were* of some sort. Fred hates cats. He doesn't trust them. I don't know what I'll do if he..." I couldn't express more. The thought of him out of my life was more heartbreaking than Weasel's torture.

Piper looked at my face and saw my truth. No matter how much I'd fought it, the truth was I'd fallen for the big wolf. I had to face it because I was going to lose it. The tears continued to fall.

"It'll be OK," she said, trying to comfort me.

But it all hit me. The shooting, the constant fear for months, the torment Weasel had subjected me to, the change my life was going to take once I'd shifted for the first time, the fear my magic wouldn't be the same, losing Fred before I had him. It was too much. I fell to the floor of the truck and curled up on the passenger side and wept my heart out. Piper pulled over somewhere, the pounding on the window seriously threatened it, and Fred leapt out, nearly ripped the door off, and pulled me into his arms. He settled himself into the passenger seat and held me as I dissolved into nothing.

Chapter 7

We pulled into an underground garage. I finally looked up. I was wrapped around Fred, trying to touch him with every part of me. I was surrounded by his scent. Salt from dried sweat, the wild, his soap—I wanted all of that on me. I felt safe and treasured. I was rubbing my face on his chest. Then I realized what I was doing—I pulled back. "Sorry." I'd probably smeared snot on him. I wiped my nose on my sleeve. It was dry, thank the lord.

His answer was to grip me tighter. I wiped my eyes. "Where are we?"

"New hideout." Fred's voice rumbled through me. He opened the passenger door and helped me out by peeling me off his lap and setting me down gently on the cement floor. I took a deep breath.

"Thank you. Thank you for finding me and saving me. I can never repay you," I said helplessly. My hands out for emphasis.

His answer was simple. "I always will."

The feeling behind the words was intense. We stared at each other for a few moments. The understanding deepened between us. The days of avoiding each other and our feelings were over. For him, this was a declaration. I nodded once and sighed. We'd see how he felt after the full moon.

"Who's garage is this?" I asked.

"Mine," Fred said. The words doubled in my mind. He included me in that single word.

His hand reached out and grasped mine. I held tight. We walked to a metal door that led into the house. Fred unlocked it, and we followed him into a modest kitchen. This wasn't a mansion like his last house. Maybe he wanted to keep this one standing or was afraid of losing another expensive house.

Piper and Fletcher followed us.

"You'll be safe here," Fred said. "Unlike my last place, no one knows this one. It's not in my name. It's old, but it's under the name of an alter ego, unlinked to me."

I looked around. The place looked old. Locked in the mid-century modern era. We walked into the living room, and Fred hurriedly pulled covers off the furniture.

"This place doesn't have modern conveniences like the internet or cable. It hasn't been upgraded since it was built in the early nineteen fifties. I've ignored it. Checked on it and made repairs as necessary, but all under another name. It should be safe as long as we stay shielded, and no one followed us.

"The plumbing and electrical work as long as you don't overwhelm the circuits with anything too powerful." He chuckled.

I moved to sit on the couch, my knees buckled just as I approached, and I sat heavily. My eyelids drooped. The weakness overwhelmed me. I sank into the couch, allowing myself to relax and bathe in the safety Fred offered. My friends were talking, but I couldn't follow anymore. I drifted to sleep.

I woke, disoriented, but warm and safe. Somehow, I'd been transported to a bed. I was no longer on an old aquamarine colored couch. I was under the covers, but Fred was laying over them in his wolf form. He was asleep. So, I took a minute and observed him. He didn't fit on the bed. His four feet hung over the side, and if he shifted around at all, he'd fall off. I wanted to laugh, but I didn't want to wake him. This was only a full-sized bed, and Fred was trying to give me all the room. He had to be terribly uncomfortable.

I smiled at him. I wanted to touch his fur, run my fingers over his velvety soft ears, but I didn't. Instead, I stretched carefully, and in so doing, realized I only wore my t-shirt and underwear. I stiffened. I wasn't ready for anyone to see me naked. Especially Fred. I was overly modest on a good day, and today wasn't one. Too much had happened to me; everything I wore was added armor. I must have moved more than I thought because Fred's eyes snapped open.

He sort of allowed himself to fall off the bed and onto his four legs, he looked at me and walked out. A few seconds later, Piper came in.

"Are you OK?" she asked.

I sighed. "Yes. I feel alright. I just panicked for a moment when I realized I'm not dressed."

She grinned. "I helped you to bed. I thought you would rest better without your pants and shoes."

I nodded. "Why was Fred in here?" That sounded mean, I wanted him here, but I needed reassurance.

"You were restless. He thought his presence made you feel safe."

He did. "Is he still out there?" I pointed to the door.

She shook her head. "He went into the garage to change back. He'll be a minute."

I looked her straight in the eye. "I think we both could have something together, but I'm not ready. I don't know how to tell him that."

She nodded. "It's OK, Bran. Just tell him. He's patient, and he has lots of time."

I shivered. I didn't want to hurt him. I still had to hurt Jed. Jed. "Piper, is Jed…?"

"He got beat up pretty bad, but Dad healed him, he's fine."

I literally sighed with relief. "I also have to let him down." I hung my head.

"Everything will be fine. Now get up, get dressed, Fred is supposed to make us breakfast."

To punctuate that, my stomach made a loud rumble, and pain

doubled me over like before. I was starved. Piper looked alarmed, but she nodded her head. She understood the feeling.

"Thanks, Pipe. Thanks for coming to save me." Emotion choked my voice.

She sat down on the bed next to me. "You're my bestie. I'll always save you, and I know you'll always save me."

I laughed. "Yeah, I'll save you from yourself." I punched her arm.

"Stop that!" She rubbed it. Like I could even hit hard enough to make her notice.

"Get off the bed and help me up."

She stood and pulled me up. I sat on the edge and stood. I still felt shaky, weak, and starving. Piper threw my pants to me, and I dressed. I could hear pans banging in the kitchen, and I knew Fred was making breakfast. The domesticity of it all brought a smile to my face. When I was ready, he'd be there. Just like he had been since I'd met him. Steady and true.

Piper walked out. I stood and pondered for a moment before I followed her. My future was a mystery, I had to hurt the two men that loved me, and I was being hunted. The weight of it all almost bore me back down to the bed.

"No," I said aloud to myself, "I will endure." I forced myself to stand tall and walk into the kitchen. I would conquer my uncertainty. I'd bend whatever changes I was going through to *my* will. I pushed my shoulders back and lifted my chin. Most importantly, I'd bring Weasel down. She'd messed with the wrong human—Branwyn Brigid O'Connor, daughter of the Celts, seer, and *witch*.

The end.

Shadow War

THE SHADOW WINGED CHRONICLES: BOOK 3

NOTE: This is an unedited sample of Shadow War, Book 3 of the Shadow Winged Chronicles.

Chapter 1

The plane bumped. Portage Pass was a little bumpy today, it had been getting cold but a warm front had pushed through bringing some mild weather and bumpy air. The man behind my seat shifted, his long legs thumping against my seat. I gritted my teeth.

Bumping my seat was a common occurrence, since the Super Cub cockpit was small, but it annoyed me to no end. I swear, one day I was going to pull the plane over and kick the shit out of one of these guys. I pulled the anger in. I wasn't really angry at my clients, just the current situation back home.

"Excuse me, miss," the man behind my seat said.

"Yeah?"

"How much longer, the turbulence makes me sick."

Just great. He hadn't better spew behind me. I hated cleaning puke out of my baby.

"Just about thirty more minutes." I pointed down at Whittier harbor in the Sound. "There's Whittier." I figured some distraction may take his mind off of the need to hurl.

"Cool, it's beautiful."

It was beautiful. The warm front had left behind some rain, maybe even some sleet, but now it was sunny and gorgeous. My client was a blacktail deer hunter heading to Montague Island in Prince William Sound southeast of the town. Whittier, enclosed as it was by the mountains and Prince William Sound, was always a stunning place, but it was more so today after the rain had cleared out the air and late summer dust and left it glittering like a jewel.

"The island is there." I pointed towards the island. It was hard to tell which one it was from here, but I was trying to reassure him. Hopefully settle him down. We were still sixty-five miles out. Not far, but far enough for an airsick passenger to make a mess of my cockpit.

The water was sapphire blue, and the trees dark green in the crystal-clear air. You could see forever today.

"That's real nice," he said.

"In the pocket of my seat, there is an airsick bag if you need it," I said. I kept some things for my passengers, ear plugs if they preferred not to connect to the intercom system with headphones, an airsick bag, snacks, sometimes a map. It just depended on the passenger.

I felt him fumble around back there and groaned to myself.

I had deliberately flown over the harbor as a sort of sightseeing experience as an extra for my clients. Now I was regretting that I didn't take the more direct route. It wasn't that much of a difference in mileage or time, but still. We hit another brief spot of turbulence, the plane bounced and juttered. My muscles clenched. Then I heard retching. Damn. The smell hit me next. I wanted to yell, but I couldn't. This was my job; the one I chose, and most days I loved it.

The air smoothed out. The rest of the flight, once we passed the land sea barrier, was smooth. I hoped he'd sealed off the bag. I banked around the island, looking for the stretch of beach I usually landed on.

Once spotted, I circled, checking for debris or trash. Montague Island was situated between the Gulf of Alaska and Prince William Sound and because of the sea currents, it collected a lot of trash from Japan. Now, it was mainly the usual stuff, fishing debris and such. A decade or more ago, it collected everything from the big Japanese tsunami and had taken years to clean up. Today, my landing spot was clear.

I banked around gently, turned into the wind and set down. The landing was ultra smooth on the wet sand. I rolled to a stop. I helped the hunter out, his legs a little shaky and scanned the area he'd been sitting for any mess. I didn't see any, so he must have hit the bag. He handed it to me. I took it without thinking. What the hell was I supposed to do with it? Ugh!

I frowned at the bag. I set it gently on the ground next to one of my Bushwheels and helped him unload. I made sure he had all the info he needed for the pick up. I took the disgusting bag of vomit, emptied my lunch from a grocery bag I had in my backpack, sealed it up in plastic, tucked it safely on the floor where it wouldn't spill or get stepped on. Then I did a brief check over the plane, and started it up. I was free the rest of the day. I took a deep breath and let it out slowly, a smile building. I sped down the beach and lifted into the air.

Since my client hadn't enjoyed my sightseeing tour, I decided to give one to myself. I had enough fuel for a leisurely cruise around the large island. I did one lazy circle, then puttered back over the other islands and over Whittier again. I flew lower than I would with a client, and watched for animals. I saw a few mountain goats in the pass, their white fur contrasting against the dark rock. We hadn't had enough snow to stick yet, so they were highly visible. I shook my head at their dexterity, and wondered what it would be like to shape one someday and crawl along the rocks on the sheer cliffs like they did.

Today was a day for the pure joy of flying. I was sad when Lake Hood came into view, but I contacted the tower, and landed anyway. If nothing was going on, I'd take to raven's wings later to continue the joy of the day.

After the plane was taken care of, I walked over to the office, turning my phone on as I went. Once it had booted up, a cacophony of sounds lit up the phone as texts and voicemail notifications hit it. I groaned. No more fun for me. Something bad must have happened. I opened the office door and went in. Dad wasn't there, so he was either still out with clients, or done and on his way home. I sat in the office chair and started reading my texts.

The first was from Branwyn, Dad, then Fletcher. I opened Bran's first. It was vague. We'd decided not to send any real information digitally. We sent important stuff via bird shifter to keep the enemy from spying on us.

"Meet at new place."

I frowned. I wasn't sure if that was Fred's new place, or the last place we met as a group. I opened Dad's. It was the same. I saved Fletcher's for last, since that one could be personal, although considering the other two, it was probably related.

"Meet at F's."

Well at least that clarified it for me. Instead of a fun flight in my raven form, I locked up the office and headed to Fred's latest place in my truck.

After Eagle had blown up Fred's mansion to steal the artifact, Fred had taken us to this older place of his that he had kept completely off the books. It wasn't much, but it worked for the core group at least. We now had over three hundred recruits to our side, and when we wanted to meet with them, it was more of an ordeal.

I pulled into the driveway. Bran's red crossover was there. I didn't see Fletcher's vehicle or Dad's, although maybe one or both were in the garage. Dad could have flown here. I knocked on the side door, and Bran let me in. A week ago, she'd been taken by Weasel and used to test the *were* making artifact. Since Eagle hadn't recovered the part of the artifact that was gold, Weasel had decided that the only way to get it to work accurately was to use human witches as the test subjects so they could supply the missing magic from the gold.

Bran had allowed it to happen to save Fred, and she'd been put through the machine. We still didn't know if it had changed her into a *were*. Weasel and Fred had stated we wouldn't know until the next full moon which was in one more week. Bran had said she'd tried to communicate with the artifact from the inside, but didn't know if that had done anything. She did have telltale signs though. Her senses were overly sensitive. She healed almost instantly after leaving the machine. Her magic was increasing quickly. Something had definitely *happened*.

Everyone was inside. "What happened?" I demanded the second the door closed behind me.

"She came into the store again," Bran answered. She looked pale, shaky.

"Damn her." I sat down heavily on the couch next to Fletcher. "What did you do? How did you get away?"

"My manager was there, in the back. When I saw her, I told Esther to call the police, loudly so Weasel heard me. Luckily, Weasel was alone. I think she was scoping out my defenses." She looked over at Fred, who was glowering in the corner at us. "Between the police sirens, and seeing Fred, she backed off."

Since the artifact incident, Fred hadn't allowed Bran out of his sight. Something had occurred between them. Bran had told me she was interested in him, but wasn't ready for anything more, but it seemed Fred had openly decided how he felt. He followed her everywhere she went. He went to work with her every day, he followed her home. She was staying at mine and Fletcher's new house, so he'd leave her with us, but he was waiting for her every morning. It was kind of sweet.

"Fred had me file a restraining order against her." Bran added.

My eyebrows hit my hairline. I looked at him sharply. His usually stoic look was briefly interrupted by a wolfish grin.

"Smart," Fletcher said.

"Hilarious," I added. "Bet she didn't see that coming. I'd have loved being a fly on the wall when she got served."

"I don't think it's happened yet, but it should be epic," Bran said.

When I'd been stalked by my one-time date, I'd been afraid of involving the police because of my supernatural status. It was dumb, in the eyes of the law I was a law-abiding citizen with a successful business helping out the economy. However, that niggling fear had stayed in my hindbrain and I hadn't done anything legal about it. Bran was human for now, and shouldn't be afraid of the law. I hoped it helped to keep Weasel away. I doubted it would, but it may be a deterrent from public places. However, Weasel had shown she had no problem making a scene, as her attack on Bran had occurred at a very busy dinner theater.

That thought made me frown. Bran saw it. My face was an open book.

"Don't worry. I know it isn't going to stop her if she's determined. I think she likes to keep me afraid. When she really comes after me, I doubt I'll see it until it's too late."

I doubted it too. Weasel was crafty. We hadn't anticipated an attack in the middle of a crowded place. She plowed through people, killing five innocents and wounding many more. Anchorage had made the national news for "escaped zoo animals wreak havoc at local theater".

For someone who professed a hatred for humans, she understood them well. Her weasel form was ancient ice age material. Nothing that was still seen today, and still she'd pulled it off as "big cat causes deaths". At least she hadn't outed all supernaturals, even if the conspiracy sites had gone wild over the videos people had uploaded.

Fred chimed in. "I think Bran should avoid her store for a while."

I did too, but I wasn't sure she'd go for it. She could be a bit... determined. She was already shaking her head.

"I can't. Anyone taking over for me would be at risk."

"I doubt it. She isn't interested in humans," Fred said.

Bran looked thoughtful. At least when Fred spoke, she listened. I was smart enough not to chime in. If I said anything she might do the opposite. He also knew when to shut up after speaking, something I couldn't do.

"I'll talk to my manager, but I..."

Before she could finish, Dad chimed in. "Bran. You are like a daughter to me. You need to listen this time. Stay away."

That really seemed to get to her. She actually was stunned into silence. Dad rarely spoke much, and I think his worry really made her think twice.

"OK." She sighed. "Until after the full moon."

Fred folded his arms over his massive chest and nodded once. Dad gave her a brief smile.

She hesitated a moment after. "What do I do? Where do I go?" She appeared lost.

"You stay at Piper's and stay inside." Dad said.

That wasn't what she meant. "You mean for the full moon?" I interjected.

"Yeah."

I looked at Fletcher. Lost. Before anything had happened, we'd used his off-grid cabin in the wilderness northwest of Lake Iliamna, but the enemy knew about it now. It would be the first place Weasel would look for Bran. Fred had land near the cabin, but there were no facilities there. At least Fletcher had a cabin, and an outhouse. Things a city girl like Bran needed, even if she did change into a *were* of some kind.

"The cave is available," Dad said. He was worried, he wanted her close so he could watch over her, I guessed. I wanted that too.

She shook her head. "I couldn't. That would lead Weasel right to your door. Shannon and Baylee would be at risk."

"You will stay here," Fred stated firmly. We all looked at him.

I sent a worried look at Bran. She looked a little panicky. Fred also noticed.

"You will be safe here. I will watch over you. As a new *were*, you will be easy for me to control."

I knew the real reason she was panicky. She was terrified she would be a cat *were* of some kind. Weasel had put that idea in her head, and Bran had a firm belief that Fred hated cat *weres*. She was really scared of him hating *her*.

I needed to think of a solution fast. This was too much for Bran. She'd just recovered from multiple gunshot wounds, then the ordeal with the artifact. I was sure she was feeling pretty fragile.

"Ummm," I was thinking on my feet. "I know a forest service cabin close to one of my routes, we can check if it's available?" I said, uncertainty clouding my voice. It was all I could come up with quickly.

Bran perked up. She liked the idea of being in the wilderness, being away from Fred until she knew what she would be—if anything. She threw me a grateful look. I gave her a quick thumbs up.

Fred frowned. Something had changed in him when Bran had been taken. He had made a decision that she was what he wanted and his protectiveness of her had multiplied. I just wish these two would work it out. We all knew they wanted to be together. It was like pulling teeth to get them there.

"Thanks, Pipe, that would be best," Bran said.

"OK, that's settled," I announced. "I'll get the info together, and I'll take you out there."

Fred tried to interrupt, but Bran cut him off. "Thanks."

Fred glowered at me. I smiled at him. Dad stayed out of it all together. He could have insisted she spent the moon time in the cave, Mom and Baylee were gone again, Dad had set up something more permanent in the lower forty-eight for them. He was savvy enough to know something was up with Bran, but even ancient immortal beings were clueless when it came to women. I swear.

"So, what do we do about Weasel? How is she involved with Eagle?" I said, changing the subject.

Before anyone could answer, a shrill whistle blasted three times. We all covered our ears. When it was over, Fred burst into action. "That's my alarm, someone is here."

We all leapt up and started to scramble for the door into the garage. Bam! I was thrown back into a wall, dust and debris rained down on me. My head was pounding, and I couldn't hear. I reached up to my ear, it was bleeding. I shook my head, but that was a bad move. So I sent a trickle of healing power through my body, and let it do its thing. When I was better, I stood and started looking for my friends and family. Someone had blown up another one of Fred's houses. How did they find us?

I pushed aside a portion of the roof. Fletcher was dragging himself out from under a broken couch and rubble. He looked for me. When he saw I was OK, he continued to pull himself out. I lifted some of the debris from him, and he stood. He was grey from the dust. I'm sure I was too. We started to dig for the others. A burst of green light surged, and a section of the rubble lifted and parted and Dad strode out, dust free. Relieved he was OK, I started to search for Bran. I was a little less worried for her then I would have been before the artifact, but I still didn't know how tough a *were* was before they'd shifted for the first time, so I started digging where I thought she had been before the blast.

Fletcher grabbed my arm and moved me over several feet. He pointed to his nose. I nodded and sniffed. He was right, she had been blasted over here, we both started lifting rubble. Soon Fred had joined us. We uncovered Bran. Her eyes were closed, and for a brief moment I worried that she was dead. Then I saw that a slash on her cheek was healing before my eyes, and soon she opened her eyes.

"What happened?" she asked.

"Someone blew us up," I answered.

Fred helped her to her feet.

There was enough of a house standing, that it had kept out whomever had blown us up, but soon someone was going to get in. I looked around. Dad's face was stony, and his arms were crossed across his chest. I knew that look, he was concentrating, hard.

"There are multiple beings with shielded signatures coming in right now," he said.

I crouched and searched for the first one.

Fletcher was growling next to me; he was in a defensive pose as well. Fred was covering Bran who had a frown on her face. The dust was clearing, and I could see daylight streaming in from a portion of the house. I was disoriented, so I wasn't sure if it was from the front, the back or the side of the house, just that shapes dressed in black with guns were coming into the house. Dad burst into his warrior shape. A scimitar cat. He seemed to prefer that one for fighting. Fred was shifting into his half shape.

Bran looked scared. Fletcher, who couldn't change as fast, picked up a long piece of two by four from the rubble. I looked for something to use as a weapon. My best warrior form was a Urayuli, a towering hairy creature of immense strength. I shifted, and picked up a large board as well.

The enemy spotted us and started shooting. None of us were bullet proof, although dad and Fred might as well have been. Dad could heal almost instantly, and Fred could as well. Bran and Fletcher as new *weres* could also heal unless they were shooting silver. Just as the thought entered my brain, Fletcher grunted as he was hit.

"It's silver," he yelled.

I was also taking fire. My Urayuli body was densely muscled, so the bullets weren't going through me. I had to think and concentrate on my healing, so it wasn't as instant as Dad's, but it was better than the first time I'd been wounded.

"Get behind me!" Bran shouted.

I winced. She was the most vulnerable, and I still wasn't over the trauma of seeing her almost die. I glanced her way; a blue shield was blocking the shots. I picked up Fletcher and pulled him behind her. Since she'd been through the artifact, her magic seemed to be growing. Once Fletcher was safe behind her shield, I waded out into the fray again. Dad and Fred were laying out the foot soldiers with quiet, bloody, efficiency. Black clad bodies were piling up. I laid into them with my board, and added a few to the pile.

That's when I saw her. Weasel. Her totem form was odd to a modern person like me. She vaguely resembled a weasel, but she was huge. She was about the height of a lynx, but long like her modern cousins. She was medium brown, her chin and belly white. She had a lightly striped coat. Her jaws were heavier than a modern weasel and lined with wicked, sharp teeth. Her paws ended in curved and vicious claws. The humans were stumbling in the rubble, but her supple long body and grasping paws made it easy for her to slink towards us with great speed. To make matters worse, she wasn't shielding her power. The weight and mass of it was like a punch in the gut. She aimed herself directly towards Bran. I wondered, not for the first time, what her obsession with Bran was.

Bran's face was full of terror. Weasel brushed by Dad, and he snagged her with his claws. Her triangular weasel face looked surprised. Maybe she hadn't recognized Raven in his scimitar cat form? She should have felt him, but I realized he was still shielding.

They'd fought before when we rescued Bran at the lab, but maybe she hadn't realized the cat was Raven. She screamed, and they wrestled, each trying to get on top and disable their opponent. She changed shape, and another scimitar cat appeared in her place. The fight was desperate and wild. Dad's cat shifted into a huge lion. Another ice age beast? It wasn't modern and it was bigger than Weasel's cat. Again, a shift, this time she changed into a short-faced bear.

I'd battled a short-faced werebear before, and it wasn't pretty. She pinned Dad's cat, and he roared. He shifted and a giant mega-fauna moose exploded up and tossed the bear into a remaining wall. The wall collapsed over the bear, but Dad's moose form charged at Weasel again. Then they were shifting and fighting and moving too fast to follow. I couldn't watch, the shock of the two gods fighting had worn off, and we were being shot at again, black clad forms were boiling into the remaining house and we were fighting for our lives.

Fred's warrior form was decimating anything that got close. I waded in, swinging my board and knocking down opponents. They were all supernaturals. Sometimes we disabled or killed one, but most were able to get up and keep fighting. There were too many of them, and our big gun was unable to help us, involved in his own fight.

We were overwhelmed. Bran was standing arms out, a blue nimbus of light surrounding her every time a bullet struck. Fletcher was still behind her. I couldn't see a way through the soldiers. For everyone I took down, it seemed like two more took their places.

Fletcher used Bran's shield to shift. In a few moments, a silver wolf with blue eyes stood in his place. I wondered if he had a plan. I didn't. I could maybe bash my way out in this form, but that didn't help anyone else, plus there was no guarantee I'd make it with all the ammo flying around. I could use my infrasound scream, but that would freeze everyone but me and that didn't help. I hadn't learned how to use my magic, past healing, and I had no other weapons. The fight between Dad and Weasel was continuing. She was nasty and cunning, but he was quick, clever, and tricky. They seemed equally matched, so no help was coming from Dad. We needed a distraction, or another layer of destruction to get away. The goal was Bran. If I could get Bran safely away, they would leave, hopefully.

I looked around. The house was in shambles, but parts still stood. The bulk of the roof was still over the main part of the opposing force. Maybe, if I pushed the wall, the roof would collapse on them. That might give me time to grab Bran and run. It was hard to tell from my angle, but it looked like she was clear of that part of the roof. If not, I sure hoped her shield would hold. I screeched and ran at the wall. It was brick, but there was a post and I was assuming a beam above the part I aimed at. If I knocked the post and the brick away, the roof should fall. I wasn't an engineer, but it made sense since the house was already weakened by the explosion. I hit it with my shoulder.

All the strength and mass of my Urayuli body shattered the post, I continued through the brick and tumbled to my side outside of the house. I felt the shudder in my bones, and the roof came down. Black clad soldiers were still streaming in, but the roof collapse cut them off from those inside. I screamed, hitting the tone that paralyzed, and I leapt over the newly collapsed part of the house to where Bran had been. Fred and Fletcher were side by side in front of her. Soldiers were in various states of hurt, some crushed under the rubble, some frozen by my scream. I grabbed Bran and leapt up and over the broken house and outside into the woods behind it.

In a few moments, I could hear people moving around, so the effects of my scream must have faded. Soon I heard crashing behind me and knew I was being pursued. Bran was yelling, but I couldn't concentrate on what. I could run with great speed in this form. Once she realized what I was doing, I felt her magic tickle my senses and I assumed she had thrown her shield back up.

Once everyone unfroze, I could hear the sounds of pursuit. Weasel was after Bran and I knew she'd chase after us. I hoped that by getting us free of the wreckage, we'd have more room to maneuver and could make things happen in our favor. It wasn't much of a plan, but we had zero chance inside the house.

Soon, Fred's gigantic grey and tan wolf form bounded around to my side. I felt a twinge of despair at leaving Fletcher behind, but I didn't have a choice. This was the best way to save him as well.

I looked around, no Weasel. At least Dad had kept her occupied so I could get Bran away. Now I had to find somewhere for her to hide. I heard someone approaching, a quick glance showed Fletcher had caught up to us. Something loosened a little in my chest, relief he'd gotten away. Still no Weasel yet.

We were running out of this small patch of woods, and even though it was a quiet neighborhood, someone was bound to notice a bigfoot and two gigantic wolves running away with a girl. We needed a plan. I looked over at Fred, he saw the gesture and immediately responded by taking the lead, moving us back into the trees, but in an alternate direction than the one I had chosen at random. This was his neighborhood, no matter how long he'd left the house alone he probably knew where to go. I followed.

Glossary of Terms

I'm including a simple pronunciation guide. Inupiaq is complex, with sounds that don't exist in English. These are *very* approximate English versions of the actual language.

Amaroq: (Ah-ma-rok) Inupiaq word for wolf.

Amaguq: (Ah-ma-gok) Inuit wolf god.

Animal Weres: A created race from an earth predator base and Sky Person technology. The animals could shift into a human form. No additional enhancements.

Atchu: (Aht-choo) Inupiaq for "I don't know."

Atiqlik: (Ah-tik-lik) Inupiaq word for a type of hooded blouse usually made from calico with a large pocket on the front. Unisex, although women may wear a version with an attached skirt.

Hróðvitnir: (H'ro-vich-nich) Icelandic for Fenrir.

Iminauraq: (Im-in-ar-auk) Inupiaq word for a mythical race of little people.

Qanuq itpich?: (Kan-uk-it-pich) Inupiaq for "how are you?"

Quyanaqpak: (Coy-un-ahk-pak) Inupiaq for "thank you."

Shadow Clan: Groups of shadow winged usually genetically related to an animal totem. For example, Raven Clan would consist of

Glossary of Terms

the Sky Person totem that represents raven, and his children, grandchildren, great-grandchildren, etc. from human/Sky Person lineage.

Shadow Winged: Any genetic mix between the Sky People and humans.

Shaman: A Native American magic user.

Sky People: The original Native American totems. They are powerful beings that came down from the heavens and subjugated the human race for a time. Identified by the animal clan they represent, i.e., Raven, Eagle, Wolf, Salmon, Orca, etc.

Tiŋiakpak: (Tin-e-ok-pok) Inupiaq for eagle.

Tornit: (Tor-nit) Inuit word for Bigfoot.

Totem: Sky People that lead a Shadow Clan, i.e., Raven, Eagle, Wolf, etc. Could be mis-identified as a god, particularly since they have godlike powers.

Tulugaq: (Too-loo-gok) Inupiaq for raven.

Urayuli: (Oo-ra-uly) Yupik word for Bigfoot.

Uvlaalluataq: (Oov-la-loa-tok) Inupiaq for "good morning."

Weres: A created race from a human base and Sky Person technology. Originally based on ice age predators but enhanced to be larger, stronger, faster, and more efficient warriors. Can shift forms into one enhanced predator.

About the Author

Jilleen Dolbeare is the author of the Shadow Winged Chronicles, an urban fantasy series about a shape-shifting bush pilot in Alaska. And the Splintered Magic Series, about a woman rebuilding her life and learning about magic with the help of her cat.

She loves riding horses, warm ocean beaches, and long walks in the mountains, none of which she can do in the Arctic, so she writes. Her activities are riding her four-wheeler on cold ocean beaches (often frozen or covered with ice), and long walks to and from work when it's 40 below—in the dark. She does keep her stakes sharp for those vamps that show up during the 67 days of night.

Jilleen lives with her husband and two hungry cats in Alaska where she also discovered her love and admiration of the Inupiaq people and their folklore.

Piper's Logbook

Also by Jilleen Dolbeare

Splintered Magic Series:

Splinter Cat: Book .5

Splintered Magic: Book 1

Splintered Veil: Book 2

Splintered Fate: Book 3

Splintered Haven: Book 4

Splintered Secret: Book 5

Splintered Destiny: Book 6*

Shadow Winged Chronicles:

Shadow Lair: Book .5

Shadow Winged: Book 1

Shadow Wolf: Book 1.5

Shadow Strife: Book 2

Shadow Witch: Book 2.5

Shadow War: Book 3

Paranormal Portlock Detective Series (with Heather G. Harris)

The Vampire and the Case of her Dastardly Death: Book .5

The Vampire and the case of the Wayward Werewolf: Book 1*

*Forthcoming

www.ingramcontent.com/pod-product-compliance
Lightning Source LLC
Chambersburg PA
CBHW030424020425
24477CB00011B/496